PUFFIN BOOKS

COUNT BAKWERDZ ON THE CARPET
and Other Incredible Stories

With eminent visitors arriving daily, like His Uppermost Loftiness, the Hi Wun of Wealthy-Rich and His Topmost Pinnacle, the Earweego of Karnstoppe, disaster suddenly strikes the accident-prone kingdom of Incrediblania. Wicked Count Bakwerdz has tampered with the royal red carpet!

What happens to the Count and the way in which the King and Queen avoid war is hilariously described. There are twelve rib-tickling stories altogether in this collection, which Norman Hunter's army of fans will enjoy as much as they did his other books about Incrediblania: *The Dribblesome Teapots, Dust-up at the Royal Disco, The Frantic Phantom* and *The Home-made Dragon.* All are available in Puffin.

NORMAN HUNTER

Count Bakwerdz on the Carpet

AND OTHER
INCREDIBLE STORIES

Illustrated by Babette Cole

PUFFIN BOOKS

Puffin Books, Penguin Books Ltd, Harmondsworth, Middlesex, England
Penguin Books, 625 Madison Avenue, New York, New York 10022, U.S.A.
Penguin Books Australia Ltd, Ringwood, Victoria, Australia
Penguin Books Canada Ltd, 2801 John Street, Markham, Ontario, Canada L3R 1B4
Penguin Books (N.Z.) Ltd, 182–190 Wairau Road, Auckland 10, New Zealand

—

First published by The Bodley Head Ltd 1979
Published in Puffin Books 1982
Reprinted 1983

—

—

'The Absent Present' was first published in *Cricket*, January 1975,
and 'A Slight Touch of Disaster' first appeared in *Puffin's Pleasure*, 1976

—

Printed and bound in Great Britain by
Cox & Wyman Ltd, Reading
Set in Baskerville 11/13 (Linotron 202)

To Sonia and Rosy
for allowing me to use their names
for the two Incrediblanian Princesses

Contents

1

Count Bakwerdz on the Carpet

In the royal carpet cupboard, where they kept the special red carpet for rolling out to welcome distinguished visitors, stood the wicked Count Bakwerdz. And he wasn't there to see if the carpet needed cleaning, which it didn't as the Queen had it swept and brushed and beaten and vacuum-cleaned every other day because she couldn't bear the idea of anything not being as clean as seven whistles and five hospitals, whether it was used or not. And he wasn't there to measure it in metres to make sure it had enough yards to go round, or rather go down the steps in front of the palace. Oh no. He was there for a low-down dastardly reason. He was tampering with the royal carpet, which is one of the dastardliest things you can do in Incrediblania.

'Ha, ha, he, ho, ho!' chuckled the wicked Count under his breath in case anyone was listening at the keyhole, which they couldn't have been as there wasn't one, and anyway whoever would want to listen at the keyhole of a carpet cupboard? 'He, he!' he chuckled again. 'That will do the trick nicely. That will put the King and Queen in a fix when their imperial visitors arrive.' And he crept craftily away leaving the royal carpet all secretly tampered with.

*

Next morning the King of Incrediblania glanced out of the window to see if the postman was coming as he was expecting a nice expensive birthday present from his cousin, the Countess Gillian. It wasn't his birthday yet, but Cousin Gillian always sent birthday presents a bit early because she'd been born rather sooner than she'd expected, and couldn't bear the idea of being late for someone else's birthday.

'Oh my goodness!' cried the King, clapping his hand to his head, forgetting he had a piece of toast and marmalade in it. 'Help, disaster, S O S and everything. Their Extreme Altitudes the Emperor and Empress of Snootistan have arrived!'

'But they aren't due until tomorrow,' said the Queen, snatching the toast and marmalade off the King's forehead and jamming them into the waste-paper basket with the gas bill. 'We aren't ready to receive them. Whatever shall we do?'

'I know, I know, I don't know!' shouted the King, running round in ovals as the room was the wrong shape for running round in circles. 'Quick, quick, summon everybody! Get royal reception committee ready. Lay out royal red carpet, call out the guard, clean the windows!'

And the Queen dashed out crying, 'Put the kettle on, dust the sideboard, change your socks everybody, hurry, hurry!'

The dastardly Count Bakwerdz was to blame. It was he who had caused the Emperor and Empress to arrive a day too soon. But how had he done it? By tampering with the royal red carpet? No, no, you can't get imperial visitors to arrive too soon however much you tamper with royal carpets. No, it was the royal calendar he'd tampered with as well. He'd put the sheet of dates for the wrong month on the calendar, but left the name of the right month at the top, and you can't get much more dastardly than that, can you? And because of that the King and Queen thought today was the sixth when it was really the seventh. They ought to have suspected something really because they'd had sausages for breakfast and they only had sausages for breakfast on the seventh of the month; the sixth was scrambled egg day. But how can kings and queens be expected to remember things like that with frightfully important emperors and empresses approaching a day too soon and nothing ready for them? Of course the Cook should have known it was the day of the Emperor's visit. The wicked Count hadn't tampered with her calendar, because he couldn't get into the kitchen without helping with the washing up, and he felt that was too undignified for a count. But oh dear, the Cook's calendar was a year-before-last one that she'd kept because she liked the picture on it.

The King was as white as a sheet just washed with super biological washing powder, except for a black streak down his nose where a speck of dust he'd wiped off the throne had stuck to his finger and come off on his face.

'Disaster, disaster!' shrieked the Queen, going whiter still as she had no black marks on her face. 'The Emperor and Empress here and no red carpet down.' She made a dash for the bell to ring for a hundred servants. The King dashed at it too and they kept dabbing each other's hands before they could get the bell push pushed.

'Emperor and -Ess coming!' shouted the King. 'Get red carpet down steps. Hurry!'

'Tell Cook to take extra pint milk, large loaf instead of small, wash best china, polish silver,' gabbled the Queen. She took a rapid look in the mirror to make sure she looked fetching, saw spots on her nose that were really on the mirror, and shot up to the purple bathroom for a quick dab with a sponge.

Before she could decide whether the spots had blown off on the way upstairs, the Lord Chamberlain burst in on the King.

'Men who put carpet down having tea with their aunties,' he gasped.

'Bother aunties,' spluttered the King. (He had

twenty-five assorted aunties of his own.) 'Must get carpet down or everything terrible!' He was too frantic to say all of his words.

'Shall lay carpet own self, Majesty,' cried the Lord Chamberlain, as he dashed out.

The King rushed round the room tearing his hair out with one hand and putting ornaments straight with the other. The Queen returned from the bathroom, saw the black mark on his nose, and wondered why he should have a smut on *his* nose just because she had seen spots on her own that weren't there.

The Lord Chamberlain grabbed some more footmen and between them they pulled the royal red carpet from the royal carpet cupboard, dragged it down and out at the front door.

The Emperor's carriage drew up at the bottom of the palace steps with imperial creakings and shoutings of 'Woa' just as the Lord Chamberlain and the footmen lugged the red carpet to the top of the enormous flight of steps leading down from the palace.

'Just'n time,' gasped the Lord Chamberlain. He grasped the end of the carpet and gave the roll a mighty push. Down went the huge roll of carpet, *bumpetty, bouncetty, bump.* But horrors! Disaster! Oo terribly er! A little spare bit of carpet came off in the Lord Chamberlain's hand and the whole great roll of carpet went bounding and bouncing uncontrolled down the steps, straight at the Emperor and Empress, who were just getting sedately out of the carriage.

'Ha, ha,' chuckled Count Bakwerdz, watching from

his grim, grey castle across the river. 'My plot succeeds. The Emperor and Empress will be furious with the King. They'll threaten war. But I shall dash up and rescue them from the runaway carpet and claim the throne. How clever of me to cut that odd bit off the carpet and so let it loose on the Emperor.' He dashed down to the river and rowed across just as the Emperor's coach drew away and the great roll of carpet came bounding down on the Emperor and Empress.

But ha! One of the Royal Incrediblanian Guards leapt at the runaway carpet and grabbed the end of it. The carpet went bounding on, unrolling as it went, down the steps and across the courtyard, past the Emperor and Empress, who stepped gracefully on to it. But before they could start going up the steps to the palace the Lord Chamberlain came tearing down to try to grab the carpet, and knocked the Royal Guard over before he could stop himself.

Horrors and disaster! The end of the carpet, let loose, started rolling itself up. Down it rolled on the Emperor and Empress, knocked them over and went on rolling with their Extreme Altitudes all wrapped up in it like the jam in a Swiss roll. Now the rampant carpet was all rolled up from its opposite end, and on it rushed down the hill towards the river with the Emperor and Empress inside it.

'Stop that carpet!' roared the King. 'Call out the guard, fetch the carpet-stoppers!'

On bounced and rolled and rumbled the runaway carpet. The townspeople joined in the chase. The guards turned out and one rather newish one, who'd put his armour on upside down in the hurry, fell into a ditch and thought he'd better stay there out of the way.

Down by the river Count Bakwerdz grabbed a bicycle that didn't belong to him and went riding to meet the carpet.

'Ha, ha!' he growled. 'This is better than I expected. Now I can stop the carpet, rescue the Emperor and Empress, and say it was a plot to kill them that I have foiled. Then with their help I shall seize the kingdom of Incrediblania.' He rang his bell, fell off the bicycle, clambered on again and pedalled off towards the rampaging carpet.

On and on rushed the carpet with imperial feet sticking out at one end and imperial heads out at the other. The Lord Chamberlain leapt on a horse to give chase, but fell off again as he didn't know how to ride.

'Call out the lifeboat!' yelled the King. 'Their Altitudes will be drowned when the carpet goes into the river.'

On went the non-stop carpet, and after it pell-mell, ding-dong, thumpetty thump what's-its-name for leather went the townspeople, the guards, the Lord Chamberlain, and the King and Queen. It zoomed down hills and round squares, into 'No Entry' streets and out of 'No Exit' ones, past the police station, the railway station, the fire station and the stationers. It took no notice of policemen with their hands up. It ignored notices that said 'Stop', or 'Diversion', or 'Road Up'.

'The river, the river!' roared the crowd. 'It's going into the river.'

Bouncetty, zoom, thump. The runaway carpet rolled on to the river's edge just as the wicked Count Bakwerdz rode up on his stolen bicycle.

'To the rescue of Their Altitudes!' he shouted, and pedalled in front of the rolling carpet.

Bong, thump, wow! The careering carpet hit the Count's bicycle and knocked it clean over the edge right into the river, Count and all. Then it stopped, right on the brinkmost brink of the wet water.

The crowd came surging up. The Lord Chamberlain and the guards carefully unrolled the carpet and let the Emperor and Empress out. The nervous guard with his armour upside down crawled out of the ditch and went home to tea.

The Emperor staggered to his feet helped by the King.

'Your Altitude,' said the King, 'what can I say?'

The Empress pushed aside the guards who were trying to help her and got up by herself.

They both looked at the King and Queen.

A distant rumble of thunder was heard.

Five volcanoes erupted in far distant lands.

An eclipse of the sun came on a fortnight too soon where nobody could see it.

The wicked Count Bakwerdz, crawling sopping wet out of the river, didn't wring his hands. He wrang himself out. And he gloated a soaking wet gloat.

'Ha, ha,' he growled, 'I've done it this time. Even
though I didn't succeed in rescuing them and so get
them on my side, they'll make war on Incrediblania
and I can join them and be appointed Governor
General when they've won.'

The King was stupefied, aghast, nonplussed, hor-
rified and desperate, all at once.

The Queen wrung her hands, rolled her eyes, shook
her head and wished she was somewhere else.

'There's going to be war,' groaned the King to himself. 'Their Altitudes will be furious, fierce, fiery and
frantically ferocious, I know they will. All is lost. Oh,
oh, oh!'

Then His Extreme Altitude the Emperor of Snootistan spoke.

'My word, old chap,' he said, 'that was a bit of a do
and no mistake. Never had such an experience in me
life, by Jove! Thoroughly enjoyed it!'

'Me too,' said the Empress, shaking carpet fluff out
of her hair-do. 'Ha, ha, wait till I tell my friends.
They'll be apple-green with envy.'

The King's mouth opened, but he didn't say anything. Words not only failed him, they disappeared
round the nearest corner. Then he recovered a bit.

'You mean you're not annoyed at being rolled down
the streets in a carpet?' he gasped. 'You mean you
aren't going to declare war on us?'

'My word, rather not,' said the Emperor. 'Don't like
wars y'know. Interfere with the sports fixtures and all
that.'

'And wars mean rationing,' said the Empress. 'No cream buns for tea. Too disaster-making.'

'But how can we apologize?' asked the King. 'How can we make up to Your Altitudes for this indignity, this terrible er er er...?'

'Not to worry,' said the Emperor. 'If it was a mistake you couldn't help it, and if you did it on purpose it was great fun.'

'Was anything said about a banquet?' enquired the Empress.

'Of course!' cried the King. He waved his hands. 'To the banqueting hall. Let there be celebrations to welcome Their Extreme Altitudes the Emperor and Empress of Snootistan.'

And a tremendously good time was had by all except the wicked Count Bakwerdz, who not only saw his plans in ruins, but had to be pegged out on his own clothes line to dry off and so couldn't go to the banquet.

'A million curses,' he growled.

Then the clothes line broke and dropped him into the muddy puddle that the drips from his clothes had made.

2

The Curious Cruise

The Queen of Incrediblania sat at the breakfast table hidden by piles of pictorial pamphlets, crowds of colourful circulars, beautiful brochures and flamboyant folders.

'You aren't going to buy more astonishing hats, are you?' asked the King. 'Where's the marmalade?'

'No, here it is,' said the Queen, answering both questions at once, and pushing the marmalade from under a ferociously coloured picture of palm trees and sand, bearing the words 'Come to the Costa del Glamoroso for sunshine, golden sands and the holiday of a lifetime'.

'I thought it was time we had the holiday of a lifetime,' went on the Queen, rummaging about among the travel brochures. 'I know some people think royalty have a lifetime of holidays, but I want to get away from all this ruling and state occasions and graciously receiving foreign potentates, not to mention laying foundation stones as if you were a hen laying concrete eggs.' She picked up a long skinny folder that opened out across the toast-rack and engulfed the coffee pot. 'How'd you like to go to the Idyllic Islands? It says here you can bathe in romantic seas, luxuriate on sun-warmed sands, play golf, go dancing and live like a lord. And you get your money back if the place goes bust before you get there.'

'Sounds fair enough,' grunted the King, 'but it doesn't appeal to me.' He didn't care for bathing because he disliked getting into water unless it was a hot bath, and even then he rather hated getting out again. Wherever he tried playing golf he got the ball through a palace window instead of down the little hole. He preferred to luxuriate in a comfortable armchair rather than on sun-warmed sand, which always got in his hair. And as for dancing, the Queen led him enough of a dance at home, and living like a king was on the whole better than living like a lord, because you didn't have to let the public see over your house for fifty pence a go with tea served in the converted stables.

'Well how about a luxury eighty-eight day cruise in the sun-kissed waters of the Mediterrwhatsit?' said the Queen, waving pictures of ships packed with excitable people and fantastic funnels.

'A cruise!' cried the King. 'That's an idea. But we don't have to go with a whole crowd of strangers. Let's go on the royal yacht.'

'It's got holes in it,' complained the Queen, 'the scuppers need scraping, the decks are disgraceful and the engines won't go.'

'I'll have all that seen to,' said the King. He rang for the Second Sea Lord, as the First Sea Lord was having breakfast in bed because it was his birthday, and gave orders to have the royal yacht mended and cleaned up, painted and polished, and made all shipshape and

Bristol fashion, while the Queen went away to choose a fetching yachting cap, highly seagoing dresses and no end of sun-bathing clothes that were designed to finish almost as soon as they began.

Then there began such a rush of work to the arms and legs aboard the royal yacht as had never been heard of. The engines were stripped down by large men, who were almost stripped down themselves, then put together again and tested amid clouds of the very best steam and nautical chuggings and plenty of dirty black grease wherever it could possibly get – which was nearly everywhere. The holes were patched up and painted over, the decks were swabbed, the brass-work polished till it hurt your eyes to look at it. And all this amid shouts of 'belay there' and 'vast heaving' and 'haul away', or 'lower away' and 'blow the man down', but this was a sea shanty sort of song and the crew didn't know the words. But they rushed about belaying and vast heaving and hauling and lowering and caulking and clenching. Everything is very difficult to understand on board ship. They don't have stairs they have companionways, the kitchen's a galley, the bedrooms are state rooms (very appropriate on a royal yacht), the back's at the stern, the front's at the bows, the scuppers go all round, and the steam comes out everywhere.

Finally there stood the royal yacht in all its magnificence. The funnel had the royal arms painted on it right the way up. There was a large sun deck covered by a fancy awning to keep the sun off. The officers were in smart white uniforms, which were mostly a bit tight through having been washed so often. The crew had bare feet so as not to damage the decks and that meant they had to clean their toe-nails as well as their finger-nails, which they thought a bit much. But on board ship you have to do as you're told instantly, or preferably before, otherwise it's mutiny and you're keel-hauled, made to walk the plank, and shot at dawn.

'Your Majesty, the royal yacht is ready for sea,' said the First Sea Lord, who'd got out of bed before breakfast this time to make the announcement himself because it made him feel as if he'd done all the getting ready, when actually he'd done nothing at all except nod his head whenever the Second Sea Lord asked if he should do something.

'Splendid,' said the King, walking across the room with a sort of rolling walk as if he was already on a ship at sea, and knocking over five fancy tables.

The next day the royal party, including the Princesses Rosy and Sonia and their husbands, Prince Egbert and Prince Poppup, and a careful selection of friends, went aboard the yacht. The gangway was raised, the ship's siren went *burp* instead of *vroooom* because something had got stuck somewhere, and the yacht moved off with the populace cheering and throwing up their hats, some of which fell in the river and were eaten by hat-eating fish.

But what about the wicked Count Bakwerdz? Surely he'd seize the throne while the King and Queen were away? Oh no he wouldn't; they'd booked him for a nice quiet holiday on a desert island, as punishment for tampering with the royal carpet and nearly annoying visiting potentates. There he could plot and gloat without doing any harm, accompanied by an armful of awful gramophone records, including one of seagull noises, and a useful book on how to embroider cushion covers with seaweed.

'I like this cruising kind of holiday,' said the Queen, reclining on an extra large deck-chair. She watched the river banks slide by and the people in the bungalows waved at her through the geraniums. Excitable ducks quacked like mad, not because it was the royal yacht, but because they hoped bits of bread would be thrown to them.

Princess Sonia spilt a teaspoonful of morning coffee on the deck, which was immediately swabbed off again by fifteen enthusiastic sailors. Princess Rosy opened a box of chocolates and a spare seagull flew off with most of them. Prince Egbert and Prince Poppup stood about admiring the scenery and hoping the scenery was admiring them.

At last evening came, which it does on board ship at the same time as it does ashore, only it doesn't seem like it because the clock is a bell that goes *dong, dong* twice when it's nine o'clock. It also goes *dong, dong* at one o'clock and five o'clock. This is most confusing and makes you feel all at sea, which the royal yacht by then almost was, as they'd come to the end of the river and that, by the laws of geography, was also the beginning of the sea.

'Stop the ship!' cried the King. 'We'll spend the evening here and go on again tomorrow.'

'Aye, aye, Majesty,' said the Captain, feeling a bit

cross at being given orders by the King, because captains on ships are supposed to be in supreme command and it shouldn't really even rain without their permission.

Ship's orders flew about. The ship's crew flew about. Bells went *dring, dring* in the engine room. The anchor went *flomp, splash* overboard and one rather new sailor nearly went with it because he got his feet tangled in the anchor cable as it went *br-r-r-r-r-*, *clank* over the side.

'Now,' said the Queen, when everything was more or less settled, 'let's have some fun. How about a firework display?'

'Good idea,' said the King.

He sent for the Captain and said, 'We are graciously pleased to have a firework display.'

'Certainly,' said the Captain, 'if Your Majesty will be graciously pleased to let me have the fireworks.'

'I don't carry fireworks about with me,' said the King. 'They might go off, then where would I be?'

'Up in the air, all in bits, or scorched to a royal cinder,' said the Captain. 'But we don't carry fireworks either in case they go off.'

'But what about rockets?' asked the King. 'You know, those things you let off when you're shipwrecked, attacked by pirates, or get a puncture, or something.'

'Oh, ah,' said the Captain, scratching his chin rather nautically. 'Yes, we've got red and green rockets, but we're only supposed to let them off in an emergency.'

'Very well,' said the Queen, coming up with a ship's bun in her hand and taking a careful bite out of it. 'Let there be an emergency. We are graciously pleased to declare an emergency. So on with the fireworks, or rather off with them. Gather round everybody,' she cried, waving her hands and letting go of the ship's bun, which made a dent in the funnel, 'we're going to have fireworks.'

'Ooooooh!' cried everybody a bit too soon, as you aren't supposed to cry 'Ooooooh!' until a rocket goes up, and anyway not until the Queen has said it first.

Over on a distant shore a coastguard put a telescope to his eye, found he couldn't see anything, then remembered to take the cap off the end of the telescope and saw the royal yacht sending up rockets.

'Shipwreck!' he shouted. 'Vessel in trouble sending up distress signals! Man the lifeboat!'

He rang the lifeboat bell and all over the little seaside town lifeboatmen who were just sitting down to a nice supper had to leave their scrambled eggs and scramble off into the lifeboat, all dressed up in waterproof coats and hats, although it wasn't raining and the sea was calm, but lifeboat rules in Incrediblania were very strict.

'They must be sinking fast,' said the lifeboat Skipper, steering like mad, 'to keep sending up rockets like that.'

'It do be the royal yacht too that it do be,' said the Assistant Skipper, shading his eyes to let him see better, which it didn't.

'We'll get royal rewards for this, boys,' cried the Skipper. And all the lifeboatmen rowed twice as fast as before to get there quicker, but they got there slower because some of them were in such a hurry to row they didn't get their oars dipped into the water.

But at last the lifeboat came alongside the royal yacht and the lifeboatmen clambered on board just as the firework display finished.

'All right, Majesty,' cried the Skipper. 'The lifeboat's here. You'll all be saved. Take it quietly now, women and children first.'

That made things difficult as there weren't any children on board, so the rescue might never have got started only the Captain managed to explain to the lifeboat Skipper that they weren't in distress or sinking or anything like that, but only having a firework display.

'I think that do be against regulations,' said the Skipper, feeling for his regulation book, but he'd left it on the mantelpiece beside the blue china cat his Aunt Aggie had given his wife. 'You shouldn't send up rockets if you aren't in distress.'

'I know that,' barked the Captain, 'but His Majesty wanted a firework display and these rockets were the only fireworks I had. I couldn't disobey His Majesty, never mind what the regulations say.'

Then the Queen swept up, all diamonds and royal smiles.

'How nice of you to come and visit us,' she said. 'You must all have nice cups of cocoa before you go back.'

The lifeboatmen said thank you very much, but they already had nice cups of tea waiting at home.

And just then a white rocket went up from the town.

'That do mean our supper's getting cold,' said the Skipper. 'Pardon us, Majesty, if we go now and glad you're not sinking.'

He bowed low, the lifeboatmen got back in the life-boat and rowed back, arriving just in time to be too late for their suppers, which had got cold and been given to their cats, so they had to make do with bread and dripping.

Next day the royal yacht got under way again and later on the King decided he'd like to take a hand at steering the ship.

'No, Majesty,' said the Captain firmly, 'I can't allow you to do that. You've got me into enough trouble with that firework display, bringing the lifeboat out for nothing. Or at least it won't be for nothing because they'll send you a bill for it, but if I let you go steering the ship, you not being a qualified seaman, Your Majesty, I'll be in trouble.'

'Nonsense,' said the First Sea Lord, coming up with his epaulettes waving in the wind. 'If His Majesty wishes to steer the ship you must let him, and I shall stand by and see that he doesn't run into anything.'

The Captain thought this a bit unnecessary, partly because he was there to stand by the King and partly because they were now at sea so there was nothing to run into.

'I don't think you ought to do it,' said the Queen,

who always believed in stopping the King from doing things in case they weren't good for him.

'I am His Imperial Majesty the King of Incrediblania,' said the King, drawing himself up to his full height and busting a button off somewhere unseen, 'and I shall be graciously pleased to steer the ship.'

He took hold of the wheel and gave it a good spin round. The royal yacht lurched to port, or else it was to starboard, then it lurched the other way, turned completely round and started zig-zagging, as if trying to dodge submarines that weren't there.

'Steady as she goes!' roared the Captain, grabbing the wheel.

'Belay there!' cried the First Sea Lord, as that was the only nautical expression he knew, though he didn't know what it meant.

The King and the Captain struggled with the wheel. The royal yacht went round in nautical circles. It passed through longitudes and latitudes. The sailors started scrubbing the decks so as to look busy in case anyone thought it was their fault.

The yacht gave another lurch. Princess Rosy upset a new box of chocolates she'd just opened, and they all rolled down the scuppers and into the sea.

'What's happening?' cried Prince Poppup, popping up through a hatch.

'Only Daddy steering the ship,' said Princess Sonia, lying back in a deck-chair and peeling a banana.

'How do you know that?' asked the Prince.

'It's the sort of thing Daddy does,' said the Princess, 'and this is the sort of thing a ship would do if he did it.' She took a polite bite of banana and wished it was dinner-time.

On went the royal yacht with the King and the Captain both trying to steer it and neither of them succeeding much. The sea, resenting it somewhat, began to get rough. Waves broke over the yacht. It took it green over the bows and white over the stern. Princess Rosy had two more boxes of chocolates washed overboard. The First Sea Lord wished he'd got a job on the underground railway where it was dryer. The Queen waved her hand and said how dare the sea be rough while she was on it. The waves waved back, but went on being rough. Dinner-time came and everyone had to have it on the floor because the yacht was pitching and tossing so much that the plates slid off the table. The sun went down, but fortunately the royal yacht didn't. It grew dark. The moon came out without asking the Queen's permission. Then it went in again as an unnecessarily large and very black cloud slid across the sky. Rain came down, lightning flashed, thunder rolled, wind whistled. Rain would have gone up, lightning would have rolled and thunder flashed, if they could.

The yacht gave a heave that made the Captain let go of the wheel.

'All right, I can manage,' shouted the King. He gave the wheel a turn.

Krump, thud, smash, wallop.

The royal yacht hit something and stopped.

'Thank goodness the sea's gone calm,' said the Queen, thinking it had.

'Shipwreck!' yelled the King. 'Lower the boats!

Abandon ship!' But nobody heard him because of all the thunder and wind.

Pandemonium took place. Shouts and screams went up. Then the thunder and lightning ceased, and the wind stopped whistling.

'Send up rockets!' cried the Captain, hoping there were some left from the firework display.

Bang, whoooosh. Up went a rocket, but nobody said 'Oooooh!' because they were too scared.

Away on the shore the coastguard looked through his telescope and shouted, 'Man the lifeboat! Ship in distress!' And he rang the lifeboat bell.

But this time the lifeboatmen didn't scramble away from their scrambled eggs because they were having sausages for supper.

'It's the royal yacht again,' said the Head Lifeboatman. 'Another of their firework displays. No need to worry, they don't want us interfering again.'

Oh, dreadful situation! The King and Queen, all the royal family and important people in danger on the royal yacht and the lifeboatmen eating sausages. The night grew darker and darker. The King looked in the ship's library for a book on what to do in case of shipwreck. The Queen tried to put on a life jacket, but it wouldn't go round her. Princess Rosy opened her last box of chocolates, but it was instantly struck by a bit of left-over lightning. Princess Sonia went to bed without getting undressed so as to be ready to be rescued. The two Princes tried to make a raft out of coffee tables, because the lifeboats had been swept away by the storm.

The last rocket went up. The last lifeboatman

finished his last sausage and went to bed. The night went on and still the royal yacht was stuck out at sea and nobody had any chance of being rescued.

If the wicked Count Bakwerdz had been free, he'd have had a great chance to seize the throne. But luckily he was still on the desert island, trying to embroider with seaweed and listening to records of 'Stormy Weather', 'Far-away Places' and 'Lonesome'.

Hours went by. Gradually the dawn began to come up just as usual, as if nothing had happened.

Then, as the King looked over the side wondering what to do, a voice said, 'Hullo!', and a gentleman with a shrimping net came walking round the yacht.

'Good gracious!' gasped the King, and everyone rushed to the side to see what was happening, except Princess Sonia, who was fast asleep dreaming of a white and pink iced Christmas.

'I must be dreaming,' said the King. But he wasn't. Could the gentleman be walking along on a submarine? No, he wasn't. Then how could he be out there walking round the royal yacht in the middle of the sea? Such things can't happen, yet this was happening.

Then the clouds drifted away, the sun came up and everything was as clear as a newly cleaned window.

The place where the royal yacht was stuck was one of those places where the tide goes out so far nobody can find it and, although they were still a long way from land, the water was quite shallow. But what with everybody being frantic and the night being so dark, they hadn't been able to see this. All they had seen was water all round them and they couldn't see it was only paddling deep.

'Everybody is to take off their shoes and stockings and paddle ashore,' ordered the Queen. They all did this, except the sailors, who didn't have shoes or stockings on and were quite used to splashing about in water anyway. The two Princes carried Princess Rosy and Princess Sonia ashore; Princess Sonia woke up, said 'Is it tea-time?' and went to sleep again. Four sailors carried the Queen ashore. The Captain sent a message to the royal palace for coaches and carriages to come and fetch everybody. Then he and the crew paddled back on board and waited for the tide to come in and float the royal yacht again which it did, according to the laws of nature that tides are very strict about obeying.

'Next time we go for a cruise we'll go by bus,' said the Queen to the King, 'and you aren't going to steer it.'

'I brought us safely ashore, didn't I?' said the King. 'If I hadn't been steering we might have been shipwrecked miles out at sea.'

The Queen didn't think there was an answer to that, or if there was she wasn't going to think about it, because a rather late, but extra sumptuous, royal breakfast was just ready.

3

What a Time!

If you wanted to know what the time was in the royal palace of Incrediblania you needed a mind like Mastermind, a brain bigger than the Brain of Britain, and be able to do mental arithmetic better than a frenzied computer.

The dining-room clock was a week and a half fast, and the drawing-room clock had been going backwards ever since the Queen's nephew came for a visit and mended it. The hall clock, which had belonged to the King's great-great-great- etc. grandmother, struck five at a quarter past one and the hands showed ten past six at twenty past eleven. The kitchen clock had only the minute hand and the Cook used it for timing her steak pies, which always came out either black as a cinder or raw as a what's-its-name.

'This is dreadful,' wailed the Queen. 'Our clocks have never been the same since we tried having British summer time. One never knows when it's a mealtime or what meal it isn't time for.' She looked at her wrist watch, but remembered it had fallen off while she was laying the foundation stone of the royal disco and was now stuck fast in no end of concrete.

'If I had to catch a train I'd be sure to miss it,' said the King, looking at the throne-room clock, which was a highly Oriental one with twisty hands so that you couldn't tell what time it was supposed to be.

The only clock that showed the right time was the town hall clock, but that was so far off you had to look through a telescope to see the time, and even it didn't work on foggy days.

'I can't stand this,' said the King. 'We shall jolly well have to buy some new clocks and never mind if they do have inflation in England.'

'You're so clever, dear,' said the Queen. 'I'll rush out and buy some clocks now.'

'No, no, stop, don't go!' cried the King. He knew once the Queen got to the shops she'd not only buy more clocks than they could do with, but also quantities of outrageous hats, astonishing dresses and frightfully expensive jewellery.

'But you know how I love shopping,' said the Queen, tickling his ear.

'Yes, yes, of course,' said the King, scratching the other ear. 'But do let's be careful. You know how easily things can get confused here. We must first of all dispose of all these outrageous clocks before we get any more. Otherwise,' he added, looking much wiser than anyone could possibly be, 'there is a danger that in getting rid of the old clocks we may get rid of the new ones by mistake. I mean there are so many people to do things in the palace.'

'I see what you mean,' said the Queen, looking at a two-yard-double-knitted cobweb in a corner of the ceiling and wondering why there weren't enough people to remove it.

'Right,' said the King. 'Call the ministers, Prince Poppup and Princess Rosy, Prince Egbert and Princess Sonia, and all the servants and we'll organize this clock disposing-of business properly.'

But although losing time is easy enough, losing clocks was so difficult as to be eleven-tenths impossible.

They put them in the palace dustbin, but the dustmen brought them round to the front door and gave them back, and had to be rewarded for being helpful.

They left them in buses and posted them with no address, but the bus people were so honest and the post office people so clever, they all came back safe and sound, with one or two other clocks that also didn't tell the time properly, which other people had managed to lose more successfully.

They tried raffling the clocks, but all the prizes got themselves won by people in the palace.

'Why doesn't Rosy draw a simply enormous dustbin with her magic crayons?' asked the King. 'Those crayons make anything she draws with them come to life. Then we could pile all the clocks in and she could rub it out and so get rid of the lot.'

'No good I'm afraid, Daddy,' said Rosy. 'I could rub out the dustbin all right, but I couldn't rub out the clocks because I hadn't drawn them.'

At last they decided the only thing to do was to have a tremendous hole dug in the palace grounds and bury all the clocks.

'Mind my crocuses!' cried the Queen anxiously, as the royal gardeners started digging the clock-hole.

'Keep off the grass!' ordered the King, talking like a public notice.

At last the clocks were all safely buried and the earth put back and patted down and some wild thyme planted, which they thought was a suitable thing to grow over old clocks.

'Right,' said the Queen, going all business-like and rubbing her hands at the thought of spending no end of money. 'Now we can all go out and buy lovely new clocks. Everyone is to get the clock they like best for their own rooms and the King and I will get the others.'

But oh dear, good gracious, and tut, tut. The sales were just finishing and all the shops were completely cleared out of clocks. Not a tick-tock to be had. Absolutely no sign of a hickory-dickory. The only watch left

nsold was the Night-watchman, who went around at
night calling 'Eleven o'clock and all's well'.

'And a lot of use that is, I'm sure,' said the Queen.
'Being woken up at all hours of the night to be told the
time when all day you have no idea at all how late or
early it is.'

'This is frightful,' agreed the King. 'Now we can't
even tell what the wrong time is.'

What a time they had, having no time. The Cook
had to time her cooking by singing verses of the
national anthem, which was very patriotic, but got a
bit boring. The Court Magician invented an eight-
hour hour-glass, like a colossal egg timer, but nobody
could lift it to turn it over. And on top of all that, a
block of flats was built in the market square and hid
the town hall clock from the palace no matter how
many telescopes you looked through.

'Why can't we have indoor sundials?' asked the
Queen. 'You know, ones that tell the time by artificial
light. Or we could invite Uncle Benjamin to stay,' she
went on. 'He's got a lovely watch that strikes the hours
and quarters, just like a pocket clock. Then we shall
always know what the time is.'

'Yes,' groaned the King, 'and we shall also always
know how his lumbago is, and how he nearly shot five
tigers on safari, and how big his sunflowers grow, and
no end of other things he keeps on talking about. If
only he had an on/off switch like the radio, we could
switch him off.'

'I rather like Uncle Ben,' said Princess Sonia. 'He
always brings me chocolates.'

So Uncle Benjamin was invited and arrived, com
plete with wonderful watch and perpetual informatio
bulletins. And the Queen got him to hang his watch
over the drawing-room mantelpiece so that everybody
could know what the time was.

Now whether it was Uncle Ben's marvellous watch
that did it by attracting its friends nobody will eve
know; but from the day Uncle Ben arrived with hi
watch, clocks of all kinds began arriving too.

The King was presented with a black marble cloc
by the West Incrediblanian Troop of Scouts whom
he'd been to inspect.

The Queen's best friend sent her a sweet little bed
side clock, as she'd just got married and been give
two alike.

The Prime Minister went to a fair and won a
alarm clock at hoop-la.

The Lord Chancellor sent off quantities of pink cir
cle stamps for a set of fish knives, but the stamp peopl
sent him a yellow and green china clock by mistake.

Several of the shops the King and Queen and roya
family had been to during the sales had new stocks o
clocks in, and sent rows and rows of them round to th
palace on approval.

The Queen won a bright blue clock with gilt legs a
a whist drive because, although she was absolutely n
use at playing cards, all the other people were eithe
less use, or thought they ought to let her win as sh
was the Queen.

The Second Footman exchanged an old pair of foot

man's breeches at the door for a cuckoo clock, and an enormous clock with illuminated hands was erected at the top of the block of flats and it chimed the hours and quarters all day and all night.

'This is worse than before,' groaned the King, clapping his hands to his ears to shut out the tick-tocking and ding-donging that was going on all over the palace. 'At least last time some of the clocks didn't work so didn't make a sound, but this is dreadful!'

Some of the clocks went a bit fast and some a bit slow, most of them struck the hours and nearly all of them chimed as well whenever they possibly could. Some had alarm bells that went off unexpectedly and made the Queen nearly climb up the curtains, and the Second Footman's cuckoo clock did more cooking than the Royal Cook.

'We must get rid of some of them, we must, we must,' cried the Queen, leaping a yard in the air as another clock bell went off without saying 'Excuse me' first.

'How on earth are we going to get rid of more clocks?' said the King. 'We can't bury them again or we shall have the palace grounds sprouting weird watches and crazy clocks.'

'I think,' said the Princess Sonia to Prince Egbert, 'that we might give this one to the Old People's Home.' She pointed to a clock that played tunes at the half hours.

'Good idea!' said Prince Egbert. 'They'll like that.'

So off they went with the clock without saying anything to anybody.

Then Princess Rosy thought it would be a good idea to get rid of another clock by presenting it to her old school, where they always made you get up frightfully early in the morning.

The Prime Minister threw his alarm clock into the lake because it woke him in the middle of the night just to show it was still working.

The Lord Chancellor dropped his yellow and green china clock while winding it and it smashed to bits.

The Second Footman took his cuckoo clock home and gave it to his old mum, who was fond of birds.

Burglars broke in and stole the King's black marble clock and the sweet little clock the Queen's married friend had sent her.

The shops sent round and collected the clocks they'd delivered on appro. thinking the King didn't like them, and the clock on gilt legs the Queen had won at whist went off with a slight bang and spread springs all over the place.

And one by one, for one reason or another, every single clock in the palace got itself disposed of. But since nobody realized the other people had got rid of their clocks, there were soon none left at all.

'This is ridiculous,' said the King, when he found out what had happened. 'First too many clocks, then none at all, then too many again, and now none at all again.'

'Shall I go out and buy some more clocks?' asked the Prime Minister helpfully.

'Pah!' snorted the King.

'Stop!' cried the Queen. 'Nobody is to go out and buy anything. We must organize this properly.'

'Oh dear,' groaned the King. 'That means a banquet, I know it means a banquet.' He knew the Queen always had banquets at the slightest excuse, because she was fond of food. He could see it all coming. A timeless banquet where every dish was got up to look like a clock. Roast cuckoo clock, alarm clock fritters, Westminster chime salad, eight-day trifle. The thought was unbearable, but fortunately he didn't have to bear it because the Queen went on:

'I know a nice little shop run by a nice little man who runs up clocks for people.'

'That's not a man, it's a mouse,' said the King. 'He lives at the Hickory-Dickory Docks.'

It was the Queen's turn to say 'Pah', but she didn't. Instead she said, 'This little shop always has one or two rather sweet clocks. We shall all go along and choose just the right clocks and not too many of them. Then we shall all know where we are. Come along.'

And before they really knew where they were the Queen had swept the King, the Princes and Princesses, the Prime Minister, the Lord Chancellor and several other officials along to her pet clock shop. It was so small they could hardly all get in, but the clock shop man made room by moving some trays of valuables out of the way.

'Good morning, Majesties, welcome, Majesties, nice day, Majesties,' gabbled the little clock man, waving his hands like a clock gone mad.

'I'm sure he's going to strike twelve,' whispered Princess Sonia.

But the little clock man struck an attitude instead and asked in his best shop manner, 'What is Your Majesty's pleasure?'

'My pleasure,' said the Queen, 'is a good fancy tea with plenty of cream cakes, but what we want from you is clocks.'

'Certainly, Majesty,' said the clock man, feeling rather glad he hadn't got to make the Queen a cake that looked like a clock, as he was absolutely useless at cooking. He disappeared into a cubby hole behind the counter and came out with a handsome clock in a glass case.

'Just the thing for the dining-room,' said the Queen. 'We'll have that.'

Then the clock man produced a gilt clock with an alarm bell that could be made to ring whenever you liked.

'The very thing for the throne-room,' said the King.

We can switch it on when we've had enough of boring foreign potentates.'

'You can get rid of boring potentates with your stories of the dragons you didn't slay, without switching on any bells,' said the Queen.

Then the Princes and Princesses and the ministers each chose a clock for various parts of the palace. The clock man promised to deliver them at once and the royal party left with becoming dignity, except that the Lord Chancellor tripped over the kerb and spilt his pocket money down a drain.

'Thank you, Majesties,' said the clock man, rubbing his hands and bowing so low he hit his forehead

on the floor and set off an alarm clock. Then he put u
a sign saying 'By appointment to Their Majesties th
King and Queen of Incrediblania', and went in t
have a minute steak for his supper.

'Well that's all right then,' said the Queen, whe
they all got back to the palace and the clocks arrive
and were carefully placed in the right rooms. 'No mor
trouble with time and clocks, thank goodness.'

Just then the clock on the block of flats struck nin
teen.

4

A Slight Touch of Disaster

The King of Incrediblania waved a highly fancy rolled-up letter over the breakfast table and nearly upset the Queen's marmalade.

'His Topmost Pinnacle, the Earweego of Karnstop-be is coming for a visit,' he said. 'We must do some-thing special to impress him, but what?'

'A lavish banquet,' suggested the Queen, who was definitely a one for food.

'No, no,' cried the King. 'That will mean you'll want to cook one of your disastrous dishes and that will depress, not impress, him. Ha!' The King was suddenly hit by an idea, between the bacon and the toast. 'I shall get the Court Magician to devise for us a wonderful automatic coach instead of the usual one with horses. That will show His Topmostness that elephants aren't everything.'

'But Majesty,' jabbered the Court Magician when the King told him what he wanted, 'I can't devise wonderful automatic coaches. I'm a magician not a, er, not a whatever it is that devises wonderful automa-tic coaches, but I could show His Topmostness a clever card trick.'

'Pah!' snorted the King. 'Of course you can devise a wonderful automatic carriage. Professor Branestawm can do it in a little place like England, and so can you.'

'It's surprising what you can do if you try,' said the Queen helpfully, getting her knitting in a quadruple tangle. So the Magician went off to see how surprising he could be by trying.

He started with the second best royal coach and with the help of several carpenters, one or two mechanically-minded gardeners and some carefully aimed magic spells, he at last produced a mechanical carriage that was certainly strange, whether it was wonderful or not. It went by horse-power, but without any horses. It went partly by clockwork, partly by steam, and sometimes by accident. But it went, which was something.

'Just in time!' exclaimed the King when he saw it. 'His Topmostness is due this afternoon. We shall go out for a trial run now. Fetch my best robes and the lightweight plastic crown I wear on these occasions. We shall take a state drive round the kingdom and finish up at the royal palace in time to welcome His Topmost Pinnacle.'

'It is certainly quicker than horses,' said the Queen, sitting majestically in the automatic carriage, 'but it smells rather like one of my special puddings getting burnt and sounds like breaking-up day in a teapot factory.'

'The scenery is lovely and goes by so quickly,' said the King. He leant out of the window to enjoy the view and his highly elaborate royal plastic crown blew off.

'Stop the carriage!' he cried. 'My crown has blown off.'

The Royal Coachman pulled levers and twiddled knobs, and the wonderful automatic carriage stopped with just a slight jerk that shot the Queen only half-way off her seat.

The King leapt out and went running back after the crown with the Coachman running after him and the two footmen running after the Coachman.

'Oh my royal goodness!' gasped the King, stopping at the very edge of a precipice. The Coachman and footmen ran into him and they all had to cling together to stop themselves falling over.

'Look!' cried the King. 'My crown, way down there, jammed in a cleft in the rocks. Nobody can possibly reach it.'

He staggered back to the coach. 'This is terrible,' he said. 'I can't possibly greet His Topmostness without a crown. He would be insulted, he would be angry, he would blow his Topmost top.'

'I could knit you one if there was time,' suggested the Queen helpfully.

'There isn't, and you can't, and it wouldn't be any good if you could,' said the King.

'Majesty,' said the Second Footman, running up, 'I could dash back to the palace and get Your Majesty another crown and the Coachman could drive round and round the palace grounds, pretending he couldn't stop the coach, until I can get another crown to you.'

'Wonderful!' exclaimed the King. 'Off you go. Tell the Coachman to keep driving, but for goodness sake hurry up with that other crown.'

The Second Footman dashed off in a cloud of best dust. The Coachman climbed up and started the carriage. *Clank, clank, poppety pop, bang, whizz, zim, clank, bonk, boom.* The carriage went rumbling along to the royal palace.

In front of the royal palace of Incrediblania was a bigger-than-a-football-crowd, waiting to see the King greet the Earweego of Karnstoppe. And the Topmost Pinnacle Himself was there in front of them all on the topmost top of a family-sized red, green and gold elephant.

The royal automatic carriage appeared in the distance. The bangs and pops and clanks came swiftly nearer. The royal carriage zimmed and whirred and banged up to the Earweego's elephant, and shot right past it.

'Hurray!' cried the crowd, throwing each other's hats in the air.

'He stops not and greets me not at all,' murmured the Earweego. 'Can this be strange royal courtesy because I am the Earweego of Karnstoppe, His Majesty he go and does not stop? I fear these Incrediblanian jokes they also go past me and I understand them not much.'

The royal automatic carriage swept and clanked along, round the drive and back again to the Earweego and his elephant. But again it swept past him, with the King hiding under the seat so that nobody should see he had no crown on, and the Queen waving her knitting.

'The carriage will not stop!' shouted the Coachman, waving his hands. 'Alas something wrong, cannot stop!'

'The carriage cannot be stopped!' cried the crowd, not throwing their hats up any more, as they didn't want to waste them.

'What's that?' asked the Court Magician. 'The carriage cannot be stopped? Nonsense, I'll stop it. I made it, so I can stop it.' He took a short cut across the keep-off-the-grass lawns and climbed up beside the Coachman.

'King's crown lost,' muttered the Coachman. 'Footman gone for another. Must keep carriage going until gets back. King cannot meet Topmost without crown or trouble.'

'Coo!' breathed the Magician, feeling a bit astonished at hearing the Coachman talk like a telegram, but he grasped the situation and stopped trying to grasp the stopping levers, so the coach went whizzing on.

'The Magician cannot stop the carriage,' cried the Prime Minister, as it came clanking and banging round again. 'I shall stop it. I have stopped clocks and I've stopped taking sugar in my tea, so I'm going to stop the carriage.'

He leapt on to the carriage as it went past, but the Coachman and the Magician hurriedly told him what was wrong and the carriage sped on, with the King crouched inside, counting the seconds until the Second Footman arrived with another crown, and wishing there weren't so many to count.

The Second Footman came running round the back of the palace so as not to be seen by the crowds. He jumped fences, he crawled through hedges, he fell into a puddle, and at last got to the crown jewel house.

'Quick,' he cried to the Keeper of the Jewels, 'give me another crown, the King's has blown off and he must have one to meet His Topmost Pinnacle.'

'The special plastic crown His Majesty was wearing is the only one we have,' said the Jewel Keeper. 'The real gold crown is too heavy for him to wear and too heavy for you to carry. All I can offer you is this little crown we use to crown the Queen of the May.' He took it from a velvet box and held it up.

Good gracious! It was about the size of a skinny little pork pie and had to be held on with a hat pin. But at least it was a crown.

'Right,' gasped the Second Footman, 'give it to me and I'll be off.'

'Fill in this form in triplicate,' said the Jewel Keeper, spreading out papers.

'Fill it in yourself!' cried the Footman, and snatching the crown he dashed off, just as the royal automatic carriage went round for the fifteenth time.

By now His Topmost Pinnacle, the Earweego of Karnstoppe was getting tired of sitting on his elephant waiting for the King to get out of the carriage that wouldn't stop. The elephant was getting tired too and sat down so that the Earweego of Karnstoppe was only just able to stop sliding off it.

'This is most awful for His Majesty!' he cried. 'I must rescue him. If all these important gentlemen cannot stop the mechanical carriage, who am I to try, but I shall. Come, let us do our thing as they say somewhere or other.'

He gave some orders and his elephant driver spoke suitably to the elephant, which stood up and walked with becoming dignity across in front of the royal carriage as it came banging and clanking and whirring towards them.

'Be on the down-sitting,' said the elephant driver, in elephant language.

The elephant sat down. The automatic carriage came tearing along.

'I can't run into His Topmost's elephant!' cried the Coachman. 'That will insult him even more than the King having no crown. I must reverse and go backwards.'

But oh, oh, there was no time for reversing. All the Coachman could do was pull the stopping lever and slam on the brakes. *Zimmmm, grrrrrr, crunch, poppy, pouff, thud*. The carriage skidded to a halt a quarter of an inch from the elephant.

'I make the hurrays!' cried the Earweego, throwing down a gold rope ladder and descending to greet the King. 'I am most glad I was able to rescue Your Majesties.'

'That's done it,' groaned the King inside the carriage. 'Now I'll have to greet him without a crown. Oh, oh, this means trouble in capital letters with coloured edges.'

But suddenly there came a scraping at the back of the coach, the door on the side away from the Earweego opened and the Footman oozed himself in.

'This is the only crown they had, Majesty,' he whispered.

'Quick,' gasped the King, snatching it. 'Give me one of your knitting-needles,' he whispered to the Queen. He skewered the little crown on to his hair, and stepped out with the Queen to greet the potentate.

Cheers went up from the assembled crowd. Hats were thrown up again. And His Topmost Pinnacle, the Earweego of Karnstoppe was doubly delighted, once to greet the King and Queen, and once to think he had stopped the runaway carriage. He hadn't, of course, but who was going to tell him that?

And as a handsome banquet had been prepared, and as it did not include any of the Queen's famous disasters, all was well.

As for the lost plastic crown, it was discovered by some birds, who used it for a nest. And their children were so stuck-up at being hatched in a royal crown that they wouldn't speak to the neighbours; they thought going 'cheep' sounded a bit inappropriate.

5

The King's Dragon

A messenger came galloping frantically up to the royal palace, leapt off his horse, dashed up the steps, tripped over the mat, went sliding and slithering across the floor into the throne-room, and finished up at the feet of the King and Queen.

'Urgent message, Majesty!' he gasped, waving a piece of paper.

The King took it. The Queen snatched it out of his hand, read it, shrieked, fainted, unfainted and said:

'Oh my goodness me, how awful, give the man a cup of cocoa and a bun – one of those stale ones left over from last Thursday's tea.'

'What's the matter?' asked the King. 'Is your cousin Connie coming to stay, or have your eight nieces and nephews all got the measles at once, or has the price of lipstick gone up again?'

The Queen handed him the paper and started wailing like a police siren.

'Great goodness-knows-whats!' cried the King, as he read the message. 'Another dragon has suddenly appeared and started ravaging the countryside. This is ridiculous. I thought we'd got rid of all the dragons.'

'This is one we must have missed,' said the Queen,

'but you know what this means. You'll have to go out and slay it.'

'Who, me?' gasped the King. 'I can't go out slaying dragons. Prince Poppup and Prince Egbert can do it.'

'No, they can't,' said the Queen, 'they're on holiday with Sonia and Rosy, remember. Rosy and Poppup have gone on a walking tour in Venice, and Sonia and Egbert are mountain climbing on Salisbury Plain, wherever that is. But we could send out a proclamation,' she added, reaching for the bell to summon the Royal Herald.

'No, no, no, no, no!' cried the King. 'That means the hand of a princess and half the kingdom to whoever slays the dragon. We haven't got any more princesses to marry off and we can't go giving away half the kingdom. I remember when that happened before and the kingdom was divided by a line that went through the royal palace. It was worse than a motorway. You had to have a passport and visas and things to go to the bathroom.'

'Oh dear, we can't have that,' wailed the Queen, who spent so long in the bath it seemed like a summer holiday. 'Can't the Captain of the Guard deal with the dragon? He's always waving his sword about and shouting things. He might as well do it at the dragon.'

'Impossible,' said the King. 'If he slew the dragon we'd have to give him half the kingdom. No, there's nothing for it; as you say I shall have to tackle this dragon, but I don't like it. I've had absolutely no practice.'

'Perhaps it's only a little dragon,' said the Queen hopefully.

Unfortunately the King was rather a little king and a bit on the weak side too. Even a little dragon could have swallowed him whole without having to take any indigestion tablets afterwards.

'There's only one thing for it,' said the Queen. 'We must get you strengthened up and made strong.'

'Well I suppose this is better than being on a diet when everything you like isn't good for you,' said the King after a day of being made big and strong.

They gave him huge helpings of everything, and tins of this and packets of that with ten thousand vitamins added. He finished up his lovely rice pudding and ate his toast crusts. He went to bed early and got up early. He did the most unlikely exercises that tied him in such knots that the servants had to come and untie him. He read books on dragons and how to slay them. They all said you had to be strong, but refrained from telling you how to be. He tried not eating any bananas and he tried eating nothing but bananas.

But it was all no good. Whatever he did or ate and drank, however many patent pills, potions, powders and positively repulsive prescriptions he took, he didn't get any bigger or stronger, in fact he was so worn out with all the strength-giving foods and exercises, he could hardly lift his hand to comb his hair, let alone slay a dragon.

'It wouldn't be so bad if there was a beautiful maiden held captive by the dragon so that I could save her,' said the King.

'Oh yes, it would be so bad,' said the Queen, sticking her nose up in the air a bit. 'It's enough for you to have to go out slaying dragons. I'm not having you chasing about all over the country with beautiful maidens, while I stay at home looking after the palace. What would the neighbours think?'

'If only the Court Magician was here,' said the King. 'He could make me big and strong, or give me a spell to cast at the dragon, or something.' And he went off to look for him.

But alas the Court Magician was away at a magicians' conference, where the magicians showed each other how to produce highly coloured rabbits out of hats. Of course they all knew that already, but they liked showing off and other magicians were the only people they could get to look at them, because none of them were much good at it.

'Oh, why must dragons be slain?' groaned the Queen. 'Why can't they have a quiz contest? I know the King would win that because he's always got an answer to everything whether there is one or not.'

At that moment a fairy flew in at the window.

The Queen, who'd left her spectacles somewhere she couldn't remember where, thought it was a fly and took a swipe at it. She missed and smashed a vase, but luckily it was one she didn't like much as it had been presented to her by the Society for the Abolition of Royalty, who believed in being polite to royalty even though they didn't believe in them.

'Pardon my not coming to the front door,' said the fairy. 'I couldn't find the bell.'

'I'm not surprised,' said the Queen. 'The King's

just mended it and it doesn't work, but whatever it is you're selling we don't want any. No extraordinary encyclopaedias, no astonishing washing powders that wash away the clothes and leave the stains, no free gifts that cost you the earth to get in exchange for forty thousand coupons cut off packets of breakfast food you can't stand.'

'No, no, no, no. I'm not selling anything. I'm a fairy.'

'I thought you people were extinct.'

'You're thinking of the Dodo. Nobody can extinct us; we just un-extinct ourselves again. I heard about your trouble with the dragon and came to see if I could help.'

'Ah,' said the Queen, 'that would be very nice. Just make the King big and strong so that he can slay the dragon, and that will do very well. But you'd better make him little and weak again immediately afterwards, otherwise I shan't be able to make him do as I tell him.'

'Well,' said the fairy, sitting on her foot and thinking furiously, 'of course I can do a magic spell to help you but it might work the wrong way. You see I was a bit naughty at school and didn't learn my magic lessons properly, so being a fairy I can do magic, but I can't always be sure what will happen. I'm afraid I can't do a spell to make the King big and strong, as it might turn him into a raspberry jelly. I could produce a purple rabbit out of his hat,' she went on, 'but rabbits aren't much use at fighting dragons unless they're very fierce rabbits, and then the rabbit might slay the King too.'

The Queen was just beginning to wish the fairy only wanted to sell her some magic washing powder, when the fairy suddenly shot up in the air and flew round in rapid circles of all sizes.

'I know what I can do!' cried the fairy. 'I know, I know. You needn't worry the least bit about the King or the dragon. Just leave it all to me. Ta ta for now, and if you want to express your thanks for what I'm going to do, just send a donation to the Society for Helping Distressed Elderly Fairies.'

And with a *whiz* and a *bzzzzz* she was gone, leaving the Queen so dazed and so stuffed up with excitement wondering what it was the fairy was going to do to help the King slay the dragon, she couldn't eat her tea, which was most unusual as she usually had three teas, one after the other.

Meantime news came in that the dragon had stamped on a bingo hall, but fortunately there was nobody in it at the time. It had breathed fire down a village street and burnt everybody's scrambled eggs. It had swallowed three shops full of pork pies, and was on its way to the royal palace.

'You'll have to go out and slay that dragon now this very minute!' cried the Queen to the King. 'We can't have it coming here swallowing the servants and stamping on my daffodils!' She started helping him on with his armour, but it was so heavy he fell down.

They hoisted him up on a crane and lowered him on to his horse, but the horse fell down too.

'Oh bother the armour,' panted the King. 'I'll go without it, perhaps the dragon's used to tinned food and won't touch a fresh King.'

'There's nothing to worry about,' the Queen assured him. 'A fairy told me everything will be all right.'

'Did she now?' said the King. 'And did she also tell you that you were going on a journey over strange ground, or that a dark man with two ears was going to leave a bag of gold at the bottom of the garden?'

He didn't believe in fairies much because he'd never met one. But at last the Queen got him all fixed up for dragon-slaying and off he went, while she waved her handkerchief, until a bird took it away from her and flew off to make it into a continental quilt for his nest.

Time went by, as time likes doing. Lunch-time, tea-time and dinner-time came and went without anything happening, except the Queen complaining there wasn't enough to eat. But the King didn't come home.

'I wonder how long it takes to slay a dragon?' asked the Queen.

'It depends on how big the dragon is,' said the Lord Chamberlain helpfully.

'And on how fierce it is,' added the Prime Minister.

'Not to mention how good or bad the King is at slaying it,' said the Lord Chancellor.

'Well don't mention it,' said the Queen. 'I'm worried, that's what I am. Suppose that fairy hasn't helped him after all? She didn't seem very capable.'

'Perhaps he can't find the dragon,' said the Prime Minister, who wasn't much good at finding things himself and often left his spectacles, his gloves, his umbrella or his hat in shops, cafes, concert halls, other people's gardens, and would have left them in buses, only he didn't go in them.

'Oh dear, suppose the dragon has eaten him,' wailed the Queen, rushing up and down the room putting the ornaments straight. 'Perhaps it's eaten the fairy, then she couldn't help him and it could eat him too. Oh, oh, oh!'

Night fell. Day broke. The servants smashed a second-best teapot. News came in that the dragon had been seen only a little way from the palace.

'Oh this is awful, I can't stand it!' cried the Queen. She banged her hands on the door of the room.

The door began to open.

'Kingy!' exclaimed the Queen.

But as the door swung open what should begin to come in but the awful, frightful, ghastly, terrifying head of the dragon.

'Help!' shrieked the Queen.

Slowly the horny spiked snout of the dragon came through the door.

The Prime Minister and all the not so prime ministers hid under the furniture, but it was rather skinny and left a lot of them sticking out.

Further and further into the room came the dreadful head of the dragon.

The Queen threw a spare clock at it and missed.

'Help, I'm going to be eaten, I know I am!' wailed the Queen, as the clock struck lunch-time.

The dragon's head crept closer to the Queen.

She collapsed into a chair, which collapsed under her and she fell on the floor.

'Oh dear, I'm so sorry,' said a voice.

The dragon's head fell thump on the floor. There was no dragon attached to it, only the head.

'I'm so sorry I startled you,' said a voice that sounded like the King's.

'Where are you?' cried the Queen. 'Has the dragon eaten you and are you inside its mouth or what?'

Suddenly there were two puffs of smoke, one green and one a bit dirty. Out of one came the King, and out of the other came the fairy with her hair rather untidy.

'Oh my goodness!' exclaimed the Queen. 'Whatever is all this? Dragons' heads coming in and scaring me, then puffs of smoke all over the place.'

'It's quite all right, my dear,' said the King. 'I met this er . . . that is to say I . . .'

'I told you it would be all right, Your Majesty,' said the fairy, patting her hair into shape, which made it worse. 'I knew I could help the King slay the dragon. But I couldn't make him big and strong because I never learnt spells like that at my fairy school. But what I could do was make him invisible. And I did. And he slew the dragon while it wasn't looking because there was nothing to look at.'

'Yes,' said the King. 'And I dragged the dragon's head back here to show you that I really had slain it. But I forgot I was invisible. I didn't mean to scare you.'

'And I didn't think the day would ever come when you could scare me,' said the Queen, in one of her voices which usually scared other people.

So that was all right. They had the dragon's head stuffed and gave it to the local museum, who wished they hadn't as it was so big and they had nowhere to put it except in the Museum Curator's office, and it scared him every time he went in.

6

The King's Birthday Present

'Now listen carefully with both ears,' commanded the Queen. 'Soon it will be the King's birthday. What can I give him when he already has everything I'll let him have?'

'How about a nice...' began the Prime Minister.

'No, no, he's already got one,' said the Queen.

'Well why not give him...' began the Court Magician.

'The very thing!' said the Queen. 'You shall make for him something he has never had and which I shall be pleased to let him have. Something mechanical I think. Something that whizzes and clicks and makes music. Let it look expensive, but not cost much, and get it done by his birthday or to the dungeons with you and no sugar in your tea.'

'Yes, Majesty. Of course, Majesty,' gabbled the Court Magician, and he went off to wonder how on earth he was going to do it. He looked up ancient books about mechanical marvels. He found how to make an egg-beater from an old lawn mower, and a mechanical spaghetti-eater that played pop music on church bells.

'No good,' he said. 'The King never eats spaghetti,

dislikes pop music and can't stand church bells. Ha! What's this? My word, just the thing. The amazing mechanical singing bird belonging to His Uppermost Loftiness the Hi Wun of Wealthy-Rich. A golden bird studded with jewels that sings the national anthem of Wealthy-Rich while the cage rotates. I can make a copy of it, using coloured glass for jewels, an old bird cage painted gold and an old gramophone motor to make it turn. But instead of the national anthem of Wealthy-Rich I shall make it sing "Happy Birthday to You". The King will be delighted. The Queen will be pleased and everything will be lovely.'

He put the book down and set to work at once.

'Well here we are,' said the Queen some time later. 'It's your birthday again already. Many happy returns, not that anyone need wish you that. Last time you gave yourself so many happy returns of your birthday it lasted five days.'

'Yes, my dear,' said the King, 'and I remember your previous birthday lasted seven weeks, and would have lasted longer only the kingdom ran out of chocolates.'

Just then the Lord Chamberlain rushed in with a large scroll that had just arrived at the palace.

'Aha, a birthday message,' said the King. 'What does it say?'

The Queen put the scroll to her ear and said, 'It doesn't say anything.'

'Let me see,' said the King, snatching the scroll, which unrolled half across the room.

'It's from His Uppermost Loftiness the Hi Wun of Wealthy-Rich. Listen . . .

'"To His Exquisite Majesty the King of Incrediblania,"' he read. '"Expensive Majesty . . ."'

'He means Dear Majesty,' said the Queen.

'"I send you birthday greetings and shall do myself the pleasurability of coming on a visit to you bringing the jolly wishes of all my people."'

'Oh dear!' cried the Queen. 'This is awkward. The birthday banquet is prepared, the royal birthday cake is made. Now with this Oriental gentleman turning up, probably with attendants and dancing girls, there won't be enough to go round. Never mind,' she said, suddenly having one of her ideas, 'you must just pretend to eat,' she said to the King, 'but don't really eat anything and everything will be all right.'

The King didn't think it would be all right at all, not eating anything on his birthday, but before he had time to say so there was a fanfare of trumpets and something covered with a cloth was wheeled in by the Court Magician.

'Ah,' said the Queen, 'here is my birthday present for you.' She whisked off the cloth revealing the Magician's wonderful bird in its tall gilt cage.

'Lovely!' cried the King. 'Just what I've always wanted. What is it?'

The Magician touched a switch and the gold bird began singing 'Happy Birthday to You'. But it only got as far as 'Happy bir...' when there were loud bangs on a gong and a voice announced:

'His Uppermost Loftiness the Hi Wun of Wealthy-Rich.'

'Galloping goldfish!' gasped the Court Magician, switching off his gold bird hurriedly. 'I didn't know he was coming. He'll recognize my machine as a copy of his own marvellous unique one. He'll blow His Uppermost top. There may be wars and sweet-rationing!'

He hurriedly threw the cloth over the bird and pushed it away, just as an ornamental and Oriental-looking gentleman strode in.

'Your Majesties,' he said, bowing low, 'most many happy come-backs of your birthday and pray accept this unimportant gift.'

He handed an elaborate casket to the King. But suddenly there were three more bangs on the gong and a voice cried, 'His Uppermost Loftiness the Hi Wun of Wealthy-Rich.'

'What, another one?' said the King.

'Don't say he's twins,' whispered the Queen, 'for we shall be even shorter of food than I feared.'

But the newcomer pointed dramatically at the first potentate.

'Guards, seize him!' he cried. 'He is an impostor. He is not the Hi Wun of Wealthy-Rich. He is the wicked Count Bakwerdz, who is plotting plots against the King.'

Guards rushed forward and in the struggle the first potentate's hat and false beard fell off, revealing the dastardly features of the wicked Count.

'But how did you know he was an impostor?' asked the King of the new potentate.

The new potentate took off his hat and beard and revealed himself as the Court Magician.

'Good gracious, it's old hey presto take a card!' cried the Queen.

'How did you know he wasn't the real Hi Wun of Wealthy-Rich?' asked the King.

'Because,' said the Magician, 'in my studies to find a suitable gift to make for Your Majesty, I found a picture of the Hi Wun and he looks quite different. He is in fact the owner of the original marvellous singing bird, of which I ventured to make a copy for the Queen to give you as a birthday present.'

'But why couldn't you have just exposed the Count? Why did you have to go dressing up in false beards and things? You make the place look like the remains of a rather wild fancy dress party.'

'But, Majesty,' protested the Magician. 'If I had burst in upon you just as you were receiving what you believed to be a highly important guest, you'd have had me thrown into the dungeons.'

'With no sugar in your tea,' added the Queen.

'Naturally,' said the Magician. 'You wouldn't have given me a chance to denounce the Count, and even if you had, you wouldn't have believed me.'

'Very likely,' said the Queen. 'With all those conjuring tricks of yours we've got quite used to not believing you.'

'Well anyway it was more exciting this way,' said the King, 'and we've caught the rascally Count. But I shall jolly well keep the present he gave me. See, this handsome casket.' He held it up.

'That's funny,' said the Magician.

'It is?' said the King. 'It doesn't make me laugh much.'

'I mean it's strange,' said the Magician. 'Why should the Count come here disguised as an important potentate and present you with a casket? He needn't have come disguised to do that.'

'Well,' said the King, 'knowing the Count, I wouldn't have accepted a casket from him in case it was a, that is to say in case it was . . . good gracious!' The casket started making a ticking noise.

'It's a bomb!' cried the Magician. 'Coming here disguised as a potentate was the Count's way of getting you to accept the casket. It's going to explode. We shall all be blown to . . .'

'Take it away!' shouted the King. He threw it to the Count, who caught it and threw it to the Queen. She caught it, though she was absolutely no good at catching things, except an occasional cold. She shrieked and threw it to the Court Magician. The casket started playing a tune. The ticking grew louder.

Tick tock, tick tick, lumty tumty, tum tum, tick tick.

'Ha, ha,' cried the Count. 'Too late. You will all be blown to . . .' He wrenched free from the guards and rushed out. The guards dashed after him. The Magician rushed to a window and flung the casket out.

Bang, crash, zoom. An explosion took place outside. So did a shriek. Smoke came in through the window. Everybody flung themselves flat on the floor, except

the Queen, who flung herself on the floor but couldn't make herself very flat.

Then came three loud bongs on the gong and a voice announced:

'His Uppermost Loftiness the Hi Wun of Wealthy-Rich.'

'Oh my goodness!' shrieked the Queen. 'Not again!'

'Well let's hope it's the genuine Hi Wun this time,' said the King, getting to his feet. 'But what a time to arrive with everyone on the floor.'

Then in came a most resplendent person, dressed in magnificent robes and dragging with him the wicked Count Bakwerdz with a blackened face and his clothes in rags.

'Greetings, Majesties,' said the Hi Wun, looking very

pleased because he thought everyone was on the floor paying their respects to him. 'Pardon the ways we are making the comings. But I find this er, er . . .'

'Ruffian,' said the Queen.

'Miscreant,' said the King.

'Scoundrel,' put in the Magician.

'Yes, all of those and some more. I find him lurking outside your palace. I feel sure you do not appreciate lurkers. And he is dressed to look like me. This too I do not appreciate, especially as he does not look like me, all dirty and ragged. But then nobody looks like me. It is not allowed.'

'No, no, yes, yes,' gabbled the King. 'You are quite right. This scoundrel is an impostor.'

'But ha, who is this?' cried the Hi Wun pointing to the Magician, who still had his Oriental robes on. 'Here is another miscreantly scoundrel trying to look like me. I will not have it. I am annoyed. I start the wars. Let there be swords and battle axes of the best quality all over the place. Permit the battles to commence. *Bang, pouff, rat a tat tat tat tat.*'

'Kindly stop talking like a second-hand machine-gun, Your Loftiness,' said the King. 'You do not understand. This ruffian you hold was trying to blow us up, but we threw the bomb out of the window and it blew up the ruffian as he escaped.'

'So,' shouted the Hi Wun. 'So you dress up someone like me to throw the bombs at someone else dressed up to look like me. I am more annoyed than ever. Let there be more wars immediately. *Bang, bang, rat tattat-tat.*'

'Oh dear,' moaned the King, 'I know we shall never be able to explain things. You see,' he spread out his hands, 'it is my birthday and . . .'

The Hi Wun flung up his hands.

'Forty thousand assorted apologies, Majesty,' he cried. 'I am so excitable with people trying to look like me I forget it is Your Esteemed birthday. I come to wish you the joyous come-agains. Pray accept this little gift.'

He let go of the Count and took from his robes a casket like the one that had exploded and handed it to the Queen.

'For you, Majesty,' he said. 'For the King I have something else.'

'Oh dear,' cried the Queen, 'I'm sure it's going to go off bang.'

The Magician rushed forward and opened the casket. It was full of jewels.

The Count grabbed it and ran off. The guards chased him. The Magician followed them. The King and Queen and the Hi Wun ran after the Magician. The Count was cornered and brought back and the Queen took the casket of jewels.

'Ha, ha, ha, he, he, he,' laughed the Hi Wun. 'This is indeed the funny stuff. I am amused. There shall not be wars. But what shall we do with this scoundrel? Let us throw him to the dragon.'

'We haven't got a dragon at the moment,' said the King.

'I should be happy to lend you one,' said the Hi Wun. 'I have an excellent model with five heads. Or possibly we could have him flung from the battlements or fired from a cannon.'

'No, no,' protested the King. 'It is my birthday and I will not have anything nasty done to anyone, not even the wicked Count Bakwerdz. Put him in the dungeon.'

'I am disappointed,' grumbled the Hi Wun. 'I feel a war coming on again.'

'No, no,' cried the King. 'I think we can show Your Loftiness something more amusing than doing nasty things to the Count. Permit me to show you the marvellous present the Queen has given me.'

'Majesty, Majesty,' whispered the Magician, all of at least ten dithers, 'as I told you, it is a copy of the Hi Wun's mechanical bird. He will be furious. There will be wars.'

'Do as I say,' whispered back the King. 'I'll think of an explanation to please him.'

The Magician went over to the singing bird and miserably pulled the cloth off.

'A golden bird that sings,' cried the Hi Wun. 'But that is a copy of my own wondrous bird. You not only make people to look like me but you make copy of my wondrous bird. I am furious. Let there be battles. Bring on the spears. *Bang, bong, rat at tattattat.*'

'Tut, tut, tut, tut, tut, tut,' said the King. 'If we must talk like machine-guns. You do not understand. This is a great compliment we pay you. Let me explain. Imitation, as the saying goes, is the sincerest flattery. So in imitating Your Loftiness we flatter you.

In imitating your wonderful machine we flatter you. Do you not like to be flattered so much?'

'Ah yes, indeed,' said the Hi Wun, coming over all pleased. 'There are customs in your curious country I shall never understand. There shall be no wars. Now let me hear your wondrous bird sing.'

The Magician pressed a lever. The bird flapped its wings and began to spin round singing 'Happy Birthday to You'. Then there was a loud click, a slight bang, a puff of smoke and the bird stopped.

'Shame,' said the Hi Wun. 'He makes the bust up. But no worryings to do because here for your birthday I have brought my own truly original wondrous singing bird.'

He clapped his hands and attendants brought in the Hi Wun's mechanical bird. It looked just like the one the Magician had made only a lot better.

'Now he sing for you,' said the Hi Wun and pressed a button.

The bird flapped its wings and began to go round and round. It opened its beak and good gracious, it sang 'Happy Birthday to You'.

'But I don't understand,' said the King, looking puzzled.

'Ah that makes the nice changes,' said the Hi Wun. 'Up to now it has been I who do not understand things.'

'But,' said the King, 'I do not understand why your wondrous bird sings "Happy Birthday to You".'

'But he does not sing happy birthday to me,' said the Hi Wun. 'He sings happy birthday to you, because it is your birthday and this is my gift to you.'

'But,' said the Queen, who thought it was about time she said something, 'I thought your wondrous bird sang the national anthem of Wealthy-Rich.'

'Yes,' said the Magician, 'that is what it said in the book I read about your wondrous bird.'

'Ah ha,' said the Hi Wun, 'now it is I who make the explainings. This tune my wondrous bird sings is the national anthem of Wealthy-Rich. It happen like this. When my little son, His Semi-Uppermost Loftiness Prince Next Wun Up, is born, the imperial orchestra play "Happy Birthday to You" and so we make that the national anthem in honour of my little son prince, and because everyone, even the least of my subjects, have to have a birthday before he or she can start being alive. It is universal custard.'

'Don't you mean custom?' said the Queen.

Before the Hi Wun could answer there came three bangs on the gong again.

'Oh for goodness sake, don't say yet another Hi Wun is arriving,' cried the King.

But the announcement simply said, 'Your Loftiness, Your Majesties, ladies and gentlemen, tea is served.'

And they all went in to have a right imperial nosh up. And they even sent a small piece of birthday cake down to the wicked Count Bakwerdz in the dungeon.

7

Ghastly Gardening

The Royal Poet to the King of Incrediblania was reading out his newest poem to the Court:

> 'Spring is here again at last,
> Everything is sprouting fast.
> Bring out spades and forks and rakes,
> Dig like everything it takes.
> Put in plants and pull up weeds,
> Sift the earth and sow the seeds.
> Soon the flowers will start to grow,
> Lovely, gorgeous, oh, oh, oh!'

'Well I must say the words are very nice,' said the Queen, who thought it was terrifically clever of anyone to make words rhyme and make them mean something as well, 'but I don't care for that poetry voice he uses. He makes it sound as if the world is going to end in ten minutes' time.'

'That gives me an idea,' said the King.

'If the world ending in ten minutes' time gives you an idea, you'd better make it an idea for not letting it end in ten minutes' time,' said the Queen. 'But I don't see how you're going to do it.'

'Pah!' snorted the King, a thing he was very good at. 'I mean all this stuff about spring and flowers sprouting gives me an idea. Let's have a gardening competition. You can have all the ministers with fair hair, I'll have all those with dark hair, and there can be a prize of fifty gold pieces for the side that grows the most and best flowers first.'

'Which side am I on?' asked the Lord Chief Inspector of Haircuts, who was bald.

'You can let off a cannon to start the competition as soon as we are ready,' said the King.

'And for goodness sake be careful where you point the thing,' said the Queen, who was nervous of cannons, except church canons, who didn't usually explode much.

'Right,' said the King, 'let us all go away and make our preparations for the flower-growing competition.'

The Queen's idea of making preparations for the flower-growing competition was to go and see the Court Magician.

'I intend to win this competition and the fifty gold pieces,' she told him.

'Of course, Majesty,' said the Magician, reckoning that no flower would have the sauce not to grow three metres high immediately if ordered to do so by the Queen.

'I want a spell or something,' said the Queen.

'Your Majesty may count the prize as won,' said the Magician, making a handkerchief disappear and pulling it out of his ear.

'Majesty would rather count it as fifty,' said the Queen, meaning gold pieces, of course.

'Magic seeds, Majesty,' said the Magician, fishing

about in a box full of nearly everything in the world and pulling out a rather second-hand looking paper packet. 'They will grow into flowers ten times as big as any others in almost no time at all.'

'I hope they do,' said the Queen, 'or you will grow into a prisoner in the new dungeons in absolutely no time at all. And not a word to the King about this. It's a deadly secret, or at least it will be deadly for you if you say a word.' And she swept out, knocking over a box that let out ten coloured rabbits, eight yards of frightful silk ribbon, and a wobbly cage full of knitted sparrows.

Meantime the King was trying to think of some way of winning the gardening competition without actually doing any work.

So he too went to see the Court Magician.

'There is to be a gardening competition,' he said, 'and I wish to be sure of winning the prize. It is my royal command that you do something about it.'

'Oh, er yes, of course, Majesty,' gabbled the Magician, going all wobbly and wondering how he was going to arrange for the King and the Queen both to win the competition.

'I daren't tell His Majesty I've given Her Majesty magic seeds,' he said to himself, 'or I shall be executed five times over, thrown into prison, burnt at the stake and dismissed without a character.'

'Well,' said the King. 'What do you propose to do?'

'I, um ar ah, I am thinking, Majesty,' said the Court Magician. And he was too. Thinking like forty-seven computers with electronic headaches.

'I can't give His Majesty more magic seeds or the Queen will be furious when she sees him planting them, and she'll know where he got them. I can't un-magic the Queen's flower seeds so that they don't grow or she'll have me flung into dungeons. But if I don't give the King something to grow enormous flowers, he'll have me flung into dungeons anyway and all this being flung into dungeons can be very bad for one. Dear me. Oh! Ah!'

Suddenly the Magician had an idea.

'Here, Your Majesty,' he said, placing a small, rather grubby tin into the King's hand, 'is some magic fertilizer. Simply sprinkle it on the earth where you have planted your seeds and your flowers will grow ten times bigger than usual in next to no time.'

'I hope they do,' said the King, 'or I'll have you planted in some very muddy ground right up to your nose in no time at all. And don't you say anything to the Queen about this or I'll have you sawn in halves like one of your own tricks and not put together again.'

He rushed out, blowing the cover off a magic cabinet, which immediately vanished itself.

'Oh dear!' gasped the Magician. 'I do hope I've done the right thing. I didn't say a word to the King about giving magic seeds to the Queen and I certainly won't say anything to the Queen about the magic fertilizer I gave to the King. But when *all* their flowers shoot up huge in no time, they'll guess I'm responsible.' He hurriedly said eighteen different spells to safeguard himself against any possible disasters and several impossible ones.

'Well that ought to make me safe against anything except the measles,' he said, 'and I had them when I was little.' And he went off to hope for the best, but not expecting it much.

Bang! The Lord Chief Inspector of Haircuts let off the starting cannon for the great flower-growing competition and startled the royal cat, who was doing some personal gardening of his own behind a bush.

'Off we go!' cried the Queen, sprinkling her seeds in a graceful curve and raking them in with a gold rake.

'Good luck to me!' cried the King, sowing his seeds in a curve the opposite way. Then he sprinkled the seeds with his magic fertilizer.

The Lord Chancellor, the Lord Chamberlain, the Prime Minister and all the other important personages sowed their seeds and raked them in, not knowing they were wasting their time, but not expecting to win the prize anyway, because they reckoned the King would pass a law disqualifying them if they did.

Then everyone rushed round with watering cans and watered the seeds nearly as well as a shower would have done if there'd been one, which there wasn't.

'We shall now have to wait several months to see whose flowers grow the biggest,' said the Royal Head Gardener, who knew all about flowers, or thought he did.

The next minute up shot the King's and Queen's flowers like a shower of rockets, twenty feet high, and they burst into blooms twice as big as jumbo-sized umbrellas.

'Good gracious!' gasped the Royal Head Gardener. He went away and would have written to someone about it, only he didn't know who to write to.

'Hurray, I've won!' cried the Queen, throwing her gold spade into the air. It came down crash on a glasshouse, but fortunately only a minor one.

'No, no, no, no!' cried the King, dancing about like a Royal Ballet dancer, only not so well. 'I've won. Those are my flowers.'

'Nonsense,' retorted the Queen, 'they're mine.'

'No, they're not, they're mine,' shouted the King.

The Lord Chancellor and the other ministers went hurriedly inside for a quiet cup of cocoa in case there should be any more spades flying about.

Suddenly the King and Queen stopped arguing.

'Help!' screamed the Queen. 'Look what's happened.'

'Oo-er,' cried the King.

For the tremendous, gigantic flowers had grown up in a circle round them. They were trapped in a floral cage, which sounds nice and romantic, but it wasn't. They couldn't get out because the stems and leaves were too thick and strong. They couldn't climb up because the frightful flowers were too high.

'Help!' they both shouted. But there was nobody to hear them. The ministers were having a jolly time over the cocoa. The Princesses and their husbands were still away. The servants were busy polishing the furniture to keep the smell of polish going, and the Court Magician had made himself invisible and gone for a holiday. The guards were all at the front of the palace, changing the guard, with so much stamping of feet and so much loud music from the band that they couldn't hear a word of the commands. But it didn't matter because they could tell from the look on the sergeant major's face what they had to do, his 'Slope arms!' face being quite different from his 'Quick march, left right, left right!' face.

'What's that?' cried the Queen, pointing to something that was coming slowly out from under a tremendous leaf.

'It's a sort of caterpillar,' said the King, 'but I've never seen a caterpillar three metres long.'

'How do you know it's three metres long?' cried the Queen. 'You haven't brought a tape measure to

measure your flowers, have you? It may be only two metres and something or other what's-their-names.'

But however big it was, it seemed to like the look of the Queen and advanced on her licking its lips.

'No, no, no, no!' cried the Queen. 'It can't eat me, caterpillars are vegetarian, aren't they?' she asked.

'I don't know what sort of caterpillar it is,' said the King. 'It must have grown enormous to match the enormous flowers.'

'Oh dear, this is worse than dragons!' cried the Queen. 'At least we can usually get them slain by offering rewards, but I don't see how we can offer half the kingdom to someone for slaying this thing, when we can't get anyone to come near us.'

The caterpillar rolled its eyes and rubbed a dozen or so of its front feet together.

Just then Prince Poppup and Princess Rosy arrived home from their walking tour in Venice with rather wet feet.

'Whatever's that in the garden?' cried Princess Rosy. 'All those enormous flowers.'

Prince Poppup ran up and peered through the stalks.

'Majesties Mum and Dad,' he cried, 'whatever are you doing there?'

'We're about to be eaten by an enormous caterpillar,' said the King. 'For goodness sake get us out of here.'

Prince Poppup drew his sword and hacked at the huge flower stems. Wow! His sword broke into three pieces, the stems were so tough.

'All right, all right,' cried Princess Rosy, as she came running out of the palace with a drawing book and her magic crayons that made things come to life when she drew them. 'I'll draw a flower-cutting-down machine and we'll soon have you out of there.'

The caterpillar crunched up half a huge leaf for starters and then advanced on the Queen again.

Princess Rosy scribbled like mad.

'Is that a flower-cutting-down machine?' asked Prince Poppup.

'I don't know what a flower-cutting-down machine looks like,' said Princess Rosy, 'but let's hope so.'

Zim. The machine came to life out of the magic crayon drawing. But it wouldn't cut the huge flower stems, it only snipped two inches off Princess Rosy's skirt. She tried again. This time her machine dug up half the lawn and vanished into the lily pond.

The caterpillar pulled a leaf off and tucked it round its neck for a napkin.

Princess Rosy scribbled out another machine. It didn't cut anything down, in fact it didn't do anything but set up the most awful noise.

And the noise brought all the ministers running out with half finished cups of cocoa. It brought all the servants running with tins of polish in their hands, ready to polish anything in sight. It even brought the guards running, half changed, but it didn't bring the Court Magician who was still on his invisible holiday.

But the guards soon made short work of the enormous flowers and the giant caterpillar, though they had a job subduing Princess Rosy's machines.

The King and Queen were saved. Hurray!

Then Princess Sonia and Prince Egbert arrived back from mountain climbing on Salisbury Plain because they couldn't find any mountains. They were too late to be of any use, but Princess Sonia came dashing in all ready to blow on any witches who were cheating around and so vanish them. But there weren't any, of course.

'Right,' said the Queen. 'Now I'll have my prize please.'

'You haven't won the prize!' protested the King. 'I've won it. My flowers were much bigger than yours!'

'No, they weren't!' said the Queen. 'Mine were far bigger, and taller.'

'They weren't!' said the King.

'Were!' said the Queen.

This 'were'/'weren't' conversation might have gone on goodness knows how long, but the Lord Chancellor said, 'Pardon, Majesties, may I make a suggestion?'

'Not if it means I haven't won the prize,' said the Queen.

'I suggest,' continued the Lord Chancellor, 'that there be two prizes each of fifty gold pieces, one for you, Your Majesty,' and he bowed low to the Queen, 'and one for you, Your Majesty,' and he bowed to the King.

'Lovely,' cried the Queen, clapping her hands so that all the servants came rushing out to see if she wanted tea served, or flowers re-arranged, or had found a speck of dust somewhere vital. But instead she ordered a magnificent banquet to celebrate the great flower-growing competition.

'And after this,' she said, during her tenth helping of pudding, 'the kind of garden I prefer is one of nice green concrete with plastic flowers stuck in it.'

8

The Absent Present

'Horrible!' said the Duke of Dulstodgy. 'Absolutely frightful, simply ghastly and not at all bearable!'

He was looking at an intensely imperial and highly ornamental inkstand that the Queen of Incrediblania had given him for Christmas. But he wasn't at all delighted, first because it was a fearsome-looking inkstand and took up so much room on the writing table there was no room to write. Second because he already had no end of inkstands, and third because he never used inkstands because he always wrote with a favourite ball-point pen his pet auntie had given him.

'I know what I'll do,' said the Duke. 'I'll send it to Connie. I never can think what to give her for Christmas.'

'Yes,' said the Duchess, 'and it will serve her right for giving us that terrible vase we can't stand the sight of and nobody seems able to break accidentally.'

So the imperial inkstand was wrapped up in acres of tissue paper with a highly ornamental card saying 'Best wishes for Christmas' and sent off to Connie, Countess of Catchmee-Iffkan. And the Duke sat down with his favourite ball-point pen and wrote to the Queen to thank her for the 'handsome and delightful inkstand'.

*

'Help!' cried the Duchess in her best screaming voice. 'This is awful. Oh my goodness, whatever can we do now?'

A message had just arrived saying that Her Majesty the Queen would be graciously pleased to come to tea that very day.

'The inkstand!' cried the Duke, clapping his hand to his head and missing it.

'Her Majesty will be furious if she doesn't see it when she comes,' gasped the Duchess.

'We must get it back at once, immediately, this very second,' roared the Duke, starting to run round in circles of various sizes. Then he stopped and sent word to Catchmee-Iffkan Castle saying would the Countess be kind enough to return the inkstand, which had been sent to her by mistake.

'Regret cannot return inkstand,' came a message back from the Countess, who always talked like a telegram because she had a nephew in the Post Office. 'Have sent to Baron Bunzanbuttah.'

'Well I do think that's a bit what's-its-name of her,' said the Duchess, 'giving our present away to someone else like that.'

'But my dear,' said the Duke, 'we gave the Queen's present to her, so we can't say anything.'

The Duchess could say a great deal, but the Duke hadn't time to listen. 'I must get the inkstand back at all costs,' he cried. 'Fetch my carriage.'

'To Bunzanbuttah Hall and drive like the devil,' he shouted, leaping into the carriage.

The driver, who wasn't quite clear how the devil might drive, started with such a jerk that the Duke was shot out of the back of the carriage and had to run like anything to catch up, which he didn't do till they'd reached the Baron's.

'Puff, puff, puff, gasp,' panted the Duke, rushing into Bunzanbuttah Hall like a second-hand whirlwind. 'Inkstand given by puff, puff, Countess by puff, gasp, pant, mistake. Must have it puff, back again.' He talked like an out of breath telegram himself, although he had no relations in the Post Office.

But alas, alack, and oh dearie dearie, tut, tut, and goodness gracious! The Baron had only that morning presented the precious inkstand to the Marquis of Mumswerd.

So off the Duke had to dash again. And he arrived at Mumswerd Mansion, panting twice as fast as before, to learn that the elusive inkstand had been passed on by the Marquis to Lady Lilly Letsgo, because he thought she was a bit special.

It was twice as far as goodness knows how far to Letsgo Lodge, but at last the Duke got there, almost in bits, flung himself in at the front door, collapsed into Lady Lilly's drawing-room, and gasped out what he wanted.

'Well, *reely*,' said Lady Lilly. 'Disgraceful I call it, you know.' She was almost invisible amongst seventy-five luxurious cushions, three pet doggies and eight kittens. 'I gave that very selfsame inkstand to the Queen my own self not so long ago. How the Marquis got hold of it I don't pretend to know...'

'Whereizzit?' panted the Duke, clawing at the carpet.

'If you really want the blessed thing,' went on Lady

Lilly, 'you'd better take it, I'm sure. Nobody else seems to appreciate it.'

She slid gracefully out of the cushions, scattering kittens and pet doggies all over the place, and slunk slitheringly into the next room, where she immediately went up in assorted screams.

The inkstand wasn't on the writing table between the brass candlesticks her Aunt Hetty had given her.

Terrible! Their Majesties would arrive at the Duke's at any moment now, and no inkstand.

'Who did you give it to?' panted the Duke. 'Tell me, quick, tell me. I must get it back. Oh, oh, oh!'

Just then in came Lord Letsgo, Lady Lilly's Grandpa. He looked at the Duke through a little eyeglass on a stick.

'Who is this er person, my dear?' he asked Lady Lilly.

'I am the Duke of Dulstodgy,' cried the Duke. 'And kindly do not look at me through little spyglass arrangements. I have come for an inkstand, which by a series of unfortunate errors was given to Lady Lilly and is now missing.'

'Oh you mean the inkstand,' said Lord Letsgo in a very high-class voice. 'Knowing that you never used it my dear, I sent it to the Queen as a little token of...'

'You sent it to the Queen!' screeched Lady Lilly and the Duke both at once, but in different voices. 'This is awful. Quick, quick to the palace!'

All three of them shot out of the house in a clump, but they were too late. They met the messenger coming out of the palace after delivering the inkstand. All was lost. They were undone.

But no. It wasn't, and they weren't. At least the Duke was a bit undone because some of his waistcoat buttons had burst off in all his hurries. But there was still a chance. Their Majesties had already left for the Duke's, and the parcel hadn't been unwrapped.

Frantically the Duke snatched it from the royal footmen, tore off the wrapping to make sure it really was the inkstand, and went rushing back to his house with the wind whistling past his ears.

Not a moment too soon. The royal coach was just drawing up at the front door. The Duke dashed round to the back and climbed in through a window, where he had a slight tussle with his own butler who thought he was a burglar and aimed a daisy one at him with a

poker. Thank goodness he missed and hit the inkstand, which was plentifully sturdy and broke the
poker, and that didn't matter as it was going to be
thrown away the next day anyway.

'At last!' gasped the Duke. He clapped the inkstand
on the writing table and dashed out to help the Duchess greet the King and Queen.

But the King and Queen hadn't come. Out of the
royal coach stepped the Lord High Equerry, who
bowed so low to the Duke and Duchess that his hat fell
off and saved him having to take it off.

'Their Majesties send their most regretful apologies,' he said. 'They have been called away on a private visit to their daughter, who has just had measles, and are therefore unable to come to tea today.'

The Duke looked at the Duchess and felt he was coming to the boil.

'Oh what a shame!' said the Duchess. 'But,' she went on, 'tea is all ready and it seems a pity to waste it, so perhaps Your Excellency would care to . . .'

The Lord High Equerry didn't wait for her to finish. He went straight in and began on the cream buns. But the Duke and Duchess didn't care. The situation was doubly saved. The inkstand was back. They'd have it chained to the writing table in case the Queen ever did call.

But the Duke can never bring himself to look at it. It makes him go all out of breath thinking of that frantic chase he needn't have done.

9

The Unlikely Picnic

The Queen of Incrediblania swept into the throne-room and blinked her eyes, because a bright golden light was shining in them.

'Disgraceful!' she cried. 'Who left the light on all night?'

'Nobody did,' said the King, coming in behind her. 'That's the sun. It's a beautiful day. I think they've sent the clouds to the cleaners.'

'Ah,' said the Queen. 'Why, so it is. A lovely day. Let's go for a picnic. All the family can come, and the ministers. We'll make it a right royal picnic with too much to eat for everyone. Even you can have what you like to eat,' she said to the King.

'Hm,' said the King, who didn't care much for picnics and would rather have had a nice enormous lunch sitting comfortably at the royal table, rather than nibbling salads and pecking at pies in the middle of a field, surrounded by resentful cows and buzzed round by hopeful wasps.

The Queen rang every bell she could find and soon the servants were rushing about packing the most enormous picnic hamper with chickens and pies and exotic jellies made in cardboard boxes specially for picnics and bottles of highly coloured lemonade. And

hen the basket was packed they had to get five foot-
en and the Royal Coachman to sit on it to get the lid
stened.

'I shall take my umbrella in case it rains, and wear a
ice summer hat in case it doesn't,' said the Queen.
he King put on a waterproof crown to be on the safe
de. The two Princes put on their most tight-fitting
ans which looked terribly smart, but were almost
mpossible to sit down in. But they reckoned they'd
ave their picnic lying down, as the Romans used to
ave their banquets, though they didn't wear tight
eans as far as the history books know. The Princesses
ut on special picnic make-up, which delayed the start
y three-quarters of an hour, but at last they were off
n the second and third best royal coaches.

Clop clop, clop clop. The coaches rolled along with the
orses making noises like coconut shells being tapped
n a board.

'Stop!' cried the King. 'This looks like a nice spot
or a picnic.'

'No, no,' said the Queen, 'just a bit further on is a
icer place with greener grass and shady trees.'

So the coaches clop clopped on and stopped again.

'Unload the food,' commanded the King.

'No, no, not yet!' cried the Queen. 'I can see somewhere much nicer over there.'

Clop clop, clopetty clop. On went the coaches.

'Here we are,' said the King. 'This is the perfect
place.'

But the Queen still wasn't satisfied. She could see a
more perfect place somewhere else.

'We shall never get anywhere at this rate,' com
plained the King, who was getting hungry and woul
have started on the picnic, but the food hamper was i
the other coach.

Seventeen times they stopped at perfect picnic spot
and seventeen times the Queen could see a better on
further on. Scenery of all kinds went past, but none o
it was quite what the Queen wanted. But at last the
arrived at a lovely green space surrounded by flower
ing bushes.

'This is it!' cried the Queen. 'Stop the coaches. Un
load the food. Let the picnic commence.'

'Wait a minute,' said the King, 'I seem to recogniz
this place. Haven't I seen that tree with the bent trun
before?'

'Don't argue,' said the Queen. 'Get the food un
packed. I'm starving.'

'I'm sure we've been here before,' said Princes
Sonia, tipping her picnic hat to a more fetching angle.

'It looks jolly handy,' said Princess Rosy. 'Why
look, there's even a seat over there, so we needn't si
on the grass.'

Then they all stopped and looked at one another.

'Ha, ha, ha, ha!' cried Princess Sonia.

'He, he, he, he!' chuckled the Princes.

'Ho, ho, ho!' laughed the King.

They discovered that they'd come back and finished
up in part of the palace grounds without realizing it.

'Well,' said the King, 'it certainly seems a nice spot.
Why don't we picnic here?'

But the Queen wouldn't hear of it. 'Picnic in the

royal grounds,' she said. 'Out of the question. Most unsuitable. Eating in the garden may be all right for some people, but it certainly isn't majestic enough for royalty.'

'Oh, all right,' said the King. 'But what do we do now? If we go off again you'll keep seeing better places a bit further on and we'll never have the picnic at all.'

'Nothing of the kind,' said the Queen. 'I have an idea. We shall drive off for half an hour and then stop, and wherever we've got to we'll have the picnic there.'

'Right, all aboard,' cried the King. And off they went. *Clopetty, clop*.

'Half an hour is up,' said the King presently. 'Stop the coaches! Here is where we picnic.'

'Oh,' said the Queen.

They'd arrived at the gas works.

'Well it might have been very handy for boiling a kettle if we'd brought a gas ring, but we haven't,' said the Queen. 'And I really don't care for all this gas while I'm eating. There'll be enough of it in the ginger beer.'

'All right,' sighed the King, 'we'll drive on for another half hour.'

So they did, and this time they stopped at the royal sewage farm. And although a farm sounds a nice place for a picnic, this kind of farm certainly wasn't.

'On again,' cried the Queen, 'and hurry up or it will be bedtime before we get there and eating in your sleep isn't good for you.'

Half an hour's more clop clopping and where were they?

Oh dear. It was the royal rubbish dump, where all the dustbins were emptied.

'The birds seem to be having a good picnic here,' said the King, 'but I don't fancy it myself.'

'Oh, this is awful!' wailed the Queen. 'Drive on and let's hope we find somewhere nice.'

They drove on. They found lovely slimy green pools. They found dried-up ponds full of old saucepans, retired bicycles and thrown-away umbrellas. They found ant heaps and wasps' nests and patches of frightful toadstools, but they couldn't find a nice place to picnic.

'Whatever's happened to everywhere?' cried the King, holding his nose because of the penetrating pong from a highly smelly mound of something countryfied. 'We ought to have stopped at some of those nice places we passed before,' he said to the Queen, 'only you kept seeing nicer places further on and now where are we?'

The Queen didn't answer, which was highly extraordinary, but she had her handkerchief over her face because of the smells.

'Drive on,' cried the King, 'and keep driving until we get somewhere more or less all right for a picnic and never mind if we can see somewhere nicer further on.'

Clop clop, clopetty clop all over again.

At last they came to a reasonable sort of meadow with no cows in it and only the smell of fresh air.

'Stop!' cried the King. 'This will have to do. Let the picnic commence!'

Then there was a confused rushing about and shouting of orders, as the ministers spread a cloth on the grass and the servants put out cushions for the Queen, and the Princesses got out all the pies and jellies and cakes and other highly eatable food.

'Here come the plates and knives and forks,' said the King, as the two Princes brought a large basket along and put it down.

The Prime Minister undid it and flung back the lid.

'Ow, ow, oh, oh, oh!' cried the Lord Chancellor.

'Now what's the matter?' grunted the King. 'Have you sat on a prickle or has a wasp kicked you or what?'

'Oh dear, oh dear,' moaned the ministers. 'Oh dreadful disaster!'

It wasn't the basket of plates and knives and forks they'd brought. It was the Queen's work-basket. In the excitement of getting ready someone had put the wrong basket on the coach.

'This is a nice state of affairs,' said the Queen, meaning the exact opposite. 'If that wicked Count Bakwerdz wasn't safely in the dungeon, I'd suspect him of doing this. Now we've found somewhere to picnic we can't eat the food. I wish I hadn't come. I knew this picnic was a mistake.'

'But it was you who suggested it,' said the King.

'What's that got to do with it?' said the Queen, picking up a large pork pie and wishing it would cut itself up, but it didn't.

'I know,' cried Prince Poppup, 'let Rosy draw knives and forks and plates and things with her magic crayons. They'll all pop up real, and we can tuck in.'

But alas Princess Rosy hadn't brought her magic crayons. She didn't think she'd need them on a picnic.

'You chaps cut the food up with your swords,' said the King to the Princes.

But of course the Princes hadn't brought their swords. One doesn't take a sword to a picnic. You don't expect to find pork pies so fierce you have to fight them, and anyway you can't eat jelly with a sword, not really elegantly.

The Queen began to wish there'd be a thunderstorm, so that the pork pie could get struck by lightning into little pieces. She tried to cut the pie with a length of cotton, the way grocers cut cheese with wire, but the pie was plentifully tough and the cotton broke.

The Lord Chancellor grabbed a bodkin and started eating peas by stabbing them one at a time. The

Minister for Foreign Affairs, who knew about China, tried to use a pair of knitting needles as chopsticks, but there wasn't anything small enough to pick up with them. Prince Egbert hacked away at a lettuce leaf with the Queen's embroidery scissors, but the lettuce leaf won easily.

'We could pass the pork pie round and each take a bite,' said the King.

'Certainly not!' cried the Queen. 'It would be most unroyal. Even if we observed the proper proro... what's-its-name and each took a bite in order of importance, it would be most, er, most...'

Before she could think what it would be most, a flock of cows came tearing across the field moo-ing like a mournful pop group. The King, Queen, Princes and

Princesses, and all the ministers dashed for the hedge and climbed through or over to get out of the way. But the cows weren't after *them*. They were after the picnic food. They gobbled up the pies without bothering that there weren't any knives and forks. They gulped down the jellies, chewed up the salad and demolished the whole picnic.

'Really!' exclaimed the Queen. 'This is too, er, too . . .'

But before she could decide what it was too, a man in a smock came rushing across the field, waving his arms and making rural noises. It was the farmer. He jumped the hedge, flung himself down in front of the King and Queen and banged his head on the ground, which made his forehead muddy.

'Oh, Majesties,' he wailed, 'please forgive this outrage, Majesties. Oh, I do be that sorry that I do be, Majesties. I do apologize for my old cows a-coming and eating up your picnic like, that I do. Please don't execute me.'

'Execute you?' said the Queen. 'We haven't got anything sharp enough to cut up a pork pie, let alone cut your head off. Anyway we don't do that sort of thing even to miscreants, rascals and villains. We just send them to distant places like Clapham Junction.'

'Please don't worry,' said the King. 'We probably shouldn't have been in your field, and we certainly couldn't eat our picnic because we'd forgotten to bring knives and forks.'

'Oh Majesty, thankee Majesty,' said the farmer, getting to his feet, 'but as my old cows do have eaten up your picnic like, I hope as how Your Majesties and everyone here will come along to the farmhouse and let my missus give ee a good farmhouse tea for to make up.'

The King and Queen said they'd be graciously pleased to let the farmer's missus do that. So they all went along to the farmhouse where the farmer's wife gave them a farmhouse tea that more than made up for everything. Even Princess Sonia let herself go on the clotted cream, though she was supposed to be slimming.

Then the royal party went back to the palace and the farmer put the royal arms on his farmhouse and a notice saying 'Purveyor of Farmhouse Teas to the Royal Household'.

'I shall have a new work-basket,' said the Queen. 'A different coloured one from the cutlery basket. It's bad enough having tried to eat pork pies with scissors and bodkins, I don't want to have to start doing needlework with knives and forks.'

10

Stop Thief!

The wicked Count Bakwerdz sat looking at himself in a mirror. The mirror looked back at him and didn't think much of what it saw, but mirrors can't help what sort of people look into them, which is a bit unfair on them.

He had been let out of the dungeon after the affair of the Hi Wun and the King's birthday present for good behaviour, which of course he had only pretended. He was only really good at doing dastardly things.

'Aha,' chuckled the Count, as he carefully fixed on a false beard and moustache. Then he altered his eyebrows and drew some lines on his face. All these made him a great deal better-looking, because you couldn't see so much of his face. But that wasn't why he was doing it. Oh no. He was scheming a direful scheme. A double-barrelled-super-cheating-roundabout plan to seize the kingdom. And it all had to do with the fact that a certain Mr Herbert Harfsole, a cobbler, looked just as the wicked Count had disguised himself to look.

But why should wicked counts disguise themselves to look like cobblers and how can that help them to steal kingdoms? That, of course, would be the sixty-four thousand dollar question if they had dollars in Incrediblania, but they didn't, so it isn't.

*

Mr Herbert Harfsole, the cobbler, was standing outside his shop in a cobbled street in Incrediblania, listening to the birds singing and wondering how they could remember always to sing the right sort of tune for whatever kind of bird they were. He was also thinking how nice it was for the street to be cobbled because that helped to wear out people's shoes, so that they had to keep bringing them to him to be mended.

Suddenly, in the midst of all these lovely thoughts there burst a most unlovely noise. Scampering of feet. Shouts of 'Stop thief!' and 'Catch him!' and 'Hi, come back you!' and 'Ho there!'.

Then round the corner came charging a man who looked exactly like Herbert Harfsole. And he was clutching a bag which he had almost certainly stolen, as bearded men don't usually carry gold handbags. Oo-er! Yes, it was the wicked Count Bakwerdz and he most certainly had stolen the gold bag, and oo even more er, it was a very important bag.

Wallop! He ran smack into Mr Harfsole. There was a rapid struggle and mix up of arms and legs and shouts of 'Let me go!', 'Got yer!' and 'Ow, oo-er!'. Then the disguised Count wrenched himself free and shot off round another corner, leaving Mr Herbert Harfsole holding the gold bag.

'Oh my goodness!' he cried, looking at the royal arms embroidered on the side of the bag. 'This must belong to the Queen. That villain must have stolen it. I can return it to the palace and get a reward. I shall . . .'

But before he had a chance to do any of these

things, the shouts and scampering feet, which had been getting nearer and nearer, arrived round the corner accompanied by a clump of guards and excited citizens.

'There he is!' they cried, pointing at Herbert. 'Grab him! He's the thief, see he has the Queen's bag!'

They swooped on Mr Harfsole, grabbed the Queen's bag from him, tied his hands with rope, put chains on his feet and bundled him into a special cart for arresting miscreants, which they'd brought with them just in case they caught the thief.

'But I'm not, I didn't,' protested Herbert Harfsole.

'Be quiet!' ordered the guards. They tied a gag round his mouth and galloped off with him to the royal palace, flung him carefully into the dungeons and took down the sign that read 'To the dungeons, Admission 10p, children half price, closed on Wednesdays'. Then they untied him, took the gag off and went away locking the door.

'Well at least they didn't charge me 10p for admission,' said Herbert to himself. 'But then I didn't really want to visit the dungeons. And I didn't steal the Queen's bag, but how am I going to tell them that when I'm locked in here?'

He banged on the dungeon door. But it was plentifully thick, and anyway everyone had gone off to a party, except the dungeon guard, who was stamping up and down some distance away and couldn't hear him, and the Royal Cook, who didn't care for parties and was playing her favourite hit tune very loudly because her ears weren't much good at listening.

Poor Herbert Harfsole! Locked in a dismal dungeon for stealing the Queen's bag when all the time it was the wicked Count Bakwerdz who had stolen it. But how was getting Herbert flung into the dungeon going to help the Count to seize the kingdom?

'This is awful,' groaned Herbert, striding up and down the rough earth floor, not caring if he did wear his shoes out because being a cobbler he didn't have to pay himself to mend them. 'I must escape somehow.'

But how? Climb out of the window. Difficult, there wasn't a window. Break down the door? Not easy, it was mighty thick and strong. Pick the lock? Doubtful, he had nothing to pick it with except a shoe horn.

'Ha!' he cried, having a sudden idea. He was going to clap his hand to his head because that's what people sometimes do when they get ideas, but it didn't seem worth while doing it in prison. 'Ha!' he cried again. 'My shoe horn. I can use it as a trowel and dig a tunnel under the floor.'

Thank goodness the floor wasn't made of enormous stone slabs or thick wooden planks or sheets of iron or obstinate bricks. It was just plain earth. Very uncomfortable for prisoners, but then prisoners are supposed to be uncomfortable.

He got down on his knees and started to dig. *Dig, dig, dig, shovel, shovel.*

'The earth's fairly soft,' he said. 'It'll take a long time to dig a tunnel, but it will keep me out of mischief, though I don't see what good it is keeping out of mischief when you get flung into dungeons just the same.' And anyway the only mischief he could get into in the dungeon was trying to escape and digging an escape tunnel wasn't keeping him out of that.

Dig, dig, dig, shovel, shovel, shovel.

Up at the palace the party was still raging. Eating, drinking and making-merry were going on, dancing was taking place, music was being played, but the King's nephew didn't think much of it. The food wasn't his idea of party food. He didn't really care for roast peacocks' ears or casseroled griffons' legs. And there were no crisps, a complete absence of ice cream and positively a lack of little sausages on sticks, all of which he liked. There were no games and he didn't feel really excited about dancing with elderly duchesses.

'I know,' said the King's nephew to himself, 'I'll go and explore the dungeons. That'll be fun!' He went along to the armoury and got the dungeon keys. Then he went down to the dungeons and unlocked the door.

Inside the dungeon Mr Harfsole was so immersed in digging he didn't notice the King's nephew. He'd dug up so many things he was beginning to think he might find buried treasure. He found old tin cans and ancient fishbones and very elderly pieces of wood, but no treasure. Nothing that the slightest bit resembled treasure.

'I say,' said the King's nephew, 'it's no use digging for treasure there, you know. We found the hidden treasure years ago and there isn't likely to be another lot.'

'I'm not really digging for treasure,' said Mr Harfsole. 'I'm digging an escape tunnel.'

'But you aren't supposed to do that,' said the King's nephew. 'You're a prisoner you know, that's why they flung you into the dungeon.'

'No, no, no, no!' cried Mr Harfsole. 'It's all a mistake. I'm innocent, that's what I am. I never did it. A miscreant stole the Queen's bag and got chased. He came rushing past me, shoved the bag into my hands and ran off. Then the guards came tearing up and grabbed me. Because I had the Queen's bag in my hand they thought I'd stolen it, but I never – I mean I didn't.'

'I say, that's jolly unfair,' said the King's nephew. 'They shouldn't have flung you into any dungeons for not stealing the Queen's bag. Here, I'll help you dig your escape tunnel, but that little shoe horn's no use. I'll go and get spades and things.'

He ran off to the garden tool shed and came back with spades and things, which he was able to do quite easily because the guards thought he was going to do some gardening.

'Righto,' he said. 'Now we can get on with it.'

Dig, dig, digetty dig. Earth and stones and occasional tin cans flew about. The piles of earth in the dungeon grew bigger and bigger as Herbert Harfsole and the King's nephew gradually disappeared from sight in the tunnel they were digging.

Dig, dig, dig. Twice Mr Harfsole dug the King's nephew up and threw him out. Three times the King's nephew threw a shovelful of earth on to Mr Harfsole instead of out of the tunnel.

'We'll soon have you out of this,' said the King's nephew, nearly shovelling Mr Harfsole out, which would have landed him back in the dungeon and that wasn't the idea.

Dig, dig, dig. Seven worms left home in great indignation. A mole who was tunnelling his way to visit his cousin turned round and went back, so as not to get dug out.

Dig, dig, dig.

At the palace the party was gradually simmering down as everyone became fuller and fuller of good things to eat. Three marchionesses went to sleep on three different sofas. Two dukes tried to tell each other the story of their lives, but as neither of them would listen it wasn't a very successful conversation.

'Let's go out and get some fresh air,' said the King. And he and the Queen went out into the royal rose garden.

'The greenfly are doing well this year,' remarked the King.

'Ridiculous,' snorted the Queen. 'Greenfly aren't supposed to do well.'

Just then along came a gardener with a greenfly-abolishing thing. He sprayed the bushes so energetically that he not only blew off most of the greenfly, but also some of the rose petals too.

'This is my favourite rose,' said the Queen, pointing to a pink one. She bent down to smell it.

Good gracious. The rose-bush seemed to be trying to go down on one knee.

'That's very respectful,' said the King. 'I didn't know rose-bushes were all that polite. They always scratch me when I try to smell the roses.'

'Help!' cried the Queen. The rose-bush wasn't trying to go down on one knee. It went down altogether and in its place up shot the King's nephew.

'Help!' shrieked the Queen again. 'Ghastly, awful!' She didn't recognize the King's nephew because his face was smothered in earth.

'That's my nephew!' exclaimed the King. 'I've often seen him with a dirty face, but never as dirty as all that.'

'What are you doing there?' demanded the Queen.

'Oh, er, sorry Auntie, Uncle, Majesties,' jabbered the nephew, brushing himself down, bowing and going red in the face, which was a waste of time as it didn't show under the dirt.

Then up came Mr Herbert Harfsole. They'd dug their tunnel right under the royal rose garden and come up under the Queen's favourite rose-bush.

'What's the meaning of this?' demanded the King. 'And who's your muddy friend and what is he doing in the royal gardens?'

'I was flung into the dungeon, Your Majesties,' explained Herbert, 'for stealing the Queen's bag. But I didn't do it.'

'That's what they all say,' said the King.

'I've never heard them,' said the Queen, who agreed with disagreeing with whatever the King said.

Then Count Bakwerdz pushed his way to the front of the crowd of guests and called out for everyone to hear:

'Listen, everyone. This poor man has been arrested and flung into the dungeon by the King for stealing the Queen's bag.'

'Hear! Hear!' cheered the dukes and marchionesses.

'But he didn't steal the bag,' shouted the Count. 'He is innocent. The King, determined to punish someone for the loss of the Queen's bag, seized this innocent man and flung him into the dungeon.'

'Shame!' cried everyone.

'It is scandalous,' continued the Count. 'Is there no

justice in Incrediblania? I demand the King and Queen abdo . . . er, abi . . ., that is to say I demand that they leave the country. I, Count Bakwerdz, will take their place and we shall have justice in the land.'

'Hurray!' shouted everyone, most of whom wanted to get back to the party never mind about anything else.

'Here wait a minute,' protested the King. 'How can you be so sure this man is innocent? He was caught with the Queen's bag in his hand.'

'Yes,' said the Count, puffing out his chest and busting a button off his coat. 'I put the Queen's bag in his hand. I stole the Queen's bag. You have imprisoned an innocent man. Therefore I demand that you hand the throne over to me.'

'Hurray!' yelled everyone again.

Oh, dreadful situation. It really looked as if the wicked Count was going to succeed at last in seizing the kingdom.

'Just a minute, not so fast, be quiet,' ordered the Queen in her most do-as-I-tell-you voice. She turned to the Count. 'How do we know you stole my bag? Do you swear you stole it? Do you swear on the honour of Incrediblania?'

'Yes, of course I do,' said the Count, 'because I did steal it and this gentleman' – he pointed to Herbert Harfsole – 'is innocent. I disguised myself to look like him because he is well known in town, then I stole the Queen's bag and pushed it into his hands. You thought he'd stolen it, but he hadn't. Ha, ha, ha, you've arrested an innocent man and thrown him into the dungeon. The country isn't going to .stand for being ruled by people who do things like that.'

Now it was the Queen's turn to say 'Aha!', and she did it in a voice that sounded like fifteen razors just out of a refrigerator.

'You,' she said, pointing a finger full of expensive rings at the Count, 'you are a criminal, sir, a criminal several times over and a criminal cannot lay claim to the throne. In fact you should be in the dungeon instead of Mr What's-his-name.'

'I, but, no, no, no,' spluttered the Count.

'Yes, yes, a goodness knows how many times yes,' said the Queen. 'First' – she tapped a finger – 'you admit to disguising yourself as this gentleman, so you are guilty of impersonation. Second' – she tapped another finger – 'you are guilty of impersonating another person with the intent to commit a felony. Third' – she tapped one more finger – 'you are guilty of stealing a handbag. Fourth' – a bit more finger tapping – 'you are guilty of stealing from the person of the sovereign and that is not only treason, it is high treason, and for that you can be executed.'

'Quite right, Your Majesty,' said the Lord Chief Justice, waving a glass of lemonade he'd brought from the party. 'He is a criminal several times over by his own confession. He must be imprisoned for life and executed at once.'

'That sounds a little difficult,' said the King, 'and anyway we don't want to go executing people. We haven't got an executioner. Just throw him into the dungeon and make him fill in the tunnel.'

'No, no, Uncle, please don't do that,' protested the King's nephew. 'We took a lot of time digging the tunnel. Please fling him into another dungeon. Let us finish the tunnel and then you can charge visitors an extra 10p to go through it.'

'Well,' said the King, scratching his chin and wishing he hadn't as his nails were a bit sharp, 'we'd better get the royal builders along to shore up the tunnel as you dig it, so that it won't fall in and bury you.'

'I'm not having tourists coming up in my rose garden,' protested the Queen.

'All right,' said the King, 'we'll have the tunnel diverted to come up somewhere else.'

So that was all arranged after a great deal of filling up of forms in triplicate and filling up of part of the tunnel, not in triplicate, and digging a branch line to come up somewhere else.

Then to make up to Mr Herbert Harfsole for being flung into the dungeon for not stealing the Queen's bag, they made him Court Cobbler and Royal Shoemaker. But he had a bit of a time with the Queen's shoes because she always found that shoes that were the right length for her feet were too narrow for them and those that were wide enough stuck out at the back.

And the wicked Count Bakwerdz went into an extra small, uncomfortable dungeon, where he was given a bent knitting-needle and a lot of tangled wool and condemned to knit frightful handbags. A proper punishment for stealing the Queen's bag.

11

The King Goes Sketching

'It's a nice fine day,' said the King of Incrediblania. 'I think I'll go down to the river and do some sketching.'

'Don't be late for lunch,' said the Queen, 'and be careful not to get your feet wet; did you change your vest this morning and why aren't there any of your handkerchiefs in the wash?'

'Pah!' said the King, who reckoned this was as good a way as any of answering those sort of questions. He picked up his gold mounted sketchbook, a nice soft pencil and a special folding stool the Court Magician had designed, which was apt to collapse if you leant over sideways a bit much.

He reached the river, sat on his sketching stool and began to sketch a steamer. He'd done one funnel and half a mast when the steamer went most inconsiderately round a bend and couldn't be seen.

'Oh bother!' thought the King. He turned over to a fresh page and began on a gentleman asleep in a chair. But a friend came along, woke the gentleman up and spoilt the picture.

'Most annoying!' said the King.

He took another new page and began to draw a sailing boat. But almost immediately the sailing boat's sails came down and there was nothing left worth drawing.

He tried to sketch a lady sitting on the grass with a sunshade, but the sunshade went down, the lady got up and walked away.

Time after time he tried to sketch something, but each time the something or somebody disappeared behind somewhere, or went off, or blew away, according to what kind of somethings or someones they were.

He even tried to sketch a little boat shed, which he reckoned couldn't very well get up and walk away. But some men came along and pulled it down.

'I'm fed up with the river,' said the King to himself. 'I shall try the country.'

He folded his stool, walked back until he came to some cows in a field. Then he opened his stool, sat down and began to draw. But the farmer opened the gate and the cows went in for their elevenses.

'This is too bad!' cried the King. 'Everything I try to sketch gets away from me. I shall go back and make a sketch of the royal palace. That can't go away and nobody is likely to pull it down.'

He sat down in the royal gardens and began to sketch the royal palace. He got confused counting the windows, then it came on to rain.

'This really is too much,' he growled. 'What's the use of being His Most Gracious Majesty the King of Incrediblania, if you can't even get a chance to sketch your own palace?'

There seemed to be no satisfactory answer to this question, so he went indoors.

'I shall do a still life drawing of that bowl of fruit,' he said, as he sat at a table in the dining-room. But the Queen came in and took the bowl of fruit away to make a fruit salad.

He tried to draw a vase of flowers, but Princess Rosy took it away to change the water. He started on a silver vase, but the Butler made off with it to polish it.

'All right,' said the King very determinedly. 'I am jolly well going to draw something and nobody is going to stop me. If I can't draw anything I can see without someone taking it away so that I can't see it, I shall draw something I can't see. I shall just imagine something.'

Then he was suddenly hit by a bright and majestic idea.

'I shall paint as well as draw,' he cried, waving his hands. 'Now I'm indoors, sitting at a nice solid table instead of perched on a perilous stool all among the grass and raindrops, I can do paintings. Much more exciting. And, of course, rather more royal.'

He got out the royal paintbox, which had so many colours in it he always had a job making up his mind which one to use and frequently got it wrong. He called to the Butler to bring him water in a crystal vase, and the Queen rushed in with last Thursday's newspaper and spread it on the table in case he made a mess, which was rather likely as painting can be a bit splashy if you get too inspired.

'Now,' said the King, thinking, and to help him think he put the paintbrush in his mouth. But that only made him say 'pwough', because he'd already

dipped it in the Prussian blue and crimson lake, which
didn't taste all that delicious.

'Now,' he said again, 'I shall be graciously pleased
to begin.'

He drew and painted the most frightful dragon, and
his painting was even more frightful than any dragon
knew how to be. He did an enchanted wood that

looked like mad macaroni doing the cancan. He
painted a moonlight scene by the river, which looked
like an overripe melon suspended over a dish of blue
custard.

'I love being an artist,' he cried, sloshing about with
the sap green and going ga ga with gamboge. 'It's
much nicer than being a king.'

He painted a ruined castle on a hill, which nearly
ruined the carpet because he kept shaking his brush
when it had too much colour in it.

He did rows of romantic windmills, each more wobbly looking than the last. He did a terrific painting of the lake in the palace grounds, which looked better upside down – but not much better.

'What are you going to do with all these paintings?' asked the Queen, who was rather good at asking awkward questions.

'Well, I er, um, ah,' said the King, who hadn't thought of that.

'It's a jolly good job you didn't use my magic crayons, Daddy,' said Princess Rosy, looking rather nervously at a row of exaggerated soldiers that the King had painted. 'I wouldn't like to see this lot come to life.'

'Majesty Dad, I have a great idea,' cried Prince Egbert. 'I know what you can do with your paintings.'

'Don't be rude!' said the Queen, sticking her nose up in the air a bit. 'Even if he is your father-in-law, he is also His Majesty the King.'

'I wasn't going to be rude, Majesty Mum,' said the Prince. 'I thought it would be a great idea to hold an exhibition of Majesty Dad's paintings.'

'Lots of people would come and see it,' said the Princess Sonia.

'And we could charge admission,' cried the King, knocking over the water, which did a very modern painting on the newspaper and on some of the carpet. 'It would make money for us, which we certainly need. Kingdoms are so expensive to run nowadays, what with PPU (Put Prices Up) Tax and all that.'

'I certainly need some new robes,' said the Queen.

'Mine are extremely last-year's looking. The last time I opened a bazaar, someone thought I was the old clothes stall.'

'Let the exhibition of my royal paintings be arranged,' cried the King, 'and send word about it to all the rich Oriental potentates. They may buy them for enormous quantities of lovely money.'

'I shall refuse to boil eggs for them,' said the Queen, remembering what happened at the Grand Congress of the Twenty Nations, when she boiled twenty-one eggs for sixty-three minutes because Cook said they needed three minutes each.

Arrangements for the Great Exhibition of Royal Paintings were in full swing and everyone was rushing round like roundabouts.

The grand gallery had been completely cleared of everything except the walls and curtains. This meant that everywhere else in the palace became rather fuller of fancy furniture than a high-class furniture shop. There were nine sumptuous settees in the King's study. Occasional tables were much more frequent than occasional in the royal drawing-room. Elegant lamps, imperial vases and majestic chairs were chin-high in the throne-room.

Then on the walls of the empty gallery the King's paintings were tastefully displayed, which caused some difficulty since some of the people who hung them couldn't bear to look at them, and the King and Queen kept having them moved because they thought they looked better somewhere else.

'We must have notices,' said the Queen. 'We can't have the public coming in here and doing as they like.'

'Let there be notices saying "No Smoking" and "Do Not Touch" and "No Dogs Admitted",' said the King.

'Don't forget some saying "No Admission" to put on our private apartments,' said the Queen. 'We can't have people rushing in on us in the middle of tea-time.'

'I don't think we ought to have just plain printed notices,' said Princess Rosy, who was inclined to be a bit on the artistic side. 'Let's make them nice and decorative.'

So she and Princess Sonia and the two Princes set to work to paint highly fancy and severely artistic notices, which were put up wherever they seemed to be needed, or wherever there was room between the King's pictures.

Finally the Great Exhibition of His Majesty's paintings was opened and the crowds poured in. Three of them. But things slackened off towards lunch-time.

'Perhaps we ought to offer prizes or say "5p off recommended price" on some of the pictures,' suggested the Queen. 'I mean we must get more people in.'

The King was all for sending soldiers out into the streets to march people into the exhibition, but fortunately the next day word had got around and the place was full and a half.

One Oriental gentleman saw a notice saying 'Entrance', pronounced it wrongly to himself, and went in expecting to be entranced by magicians, jugglers, fire eaters, and sword swallowers, but had to be content to be shown unsuccessful card tricks by the Court Magician. Another Eastern potentate nearly went into a room marked 'Ladies', expecting to see dancing girls, but was fortunately stopped by a collection of girls with freshly powdered noses, who came out in a clump and swept him away.

One or two people were slightly mystified by a notice that said 'Keep off the grass', which had got in by mistake as there was no grass except in the King's pictures and that looking like anything else but. There were also signs saying 'Cattle Crossing' and 'No Parking', which the Princesses had used to paint other notices on the opposite side of and had forgotten to cover up the first side.

'We haven't sold any pictures yet,' said the King on the second afternoon.

Then business began to brisk up.

Someone bought a very tasty notice painted by Princess Rosy that said 'Please leave sticks and umbrellas at the entrance', surrounded by pink roses and very imaginative daisies.

Three of Princess Sonia's 'No Smoking' notices ornamented with tongues of fire and green blackbirds were snapped up at quite exciting prices and an Eastern potentate wanted to buy one of the windows because he thought the view of the royal rose garden was a picture, which it certainly was, but not in the way he meant.

'Nobody's buying any of my pictures,' complained the King.

So Princess Rosy painted a very fetching notice with the royal arms surrounded by mauve daffodils that said 'Must be sold' and hung it by the King's pictures.

'Nobody can ignore that,' she said. 'It's a royal command. They're bound to buy your pictures now.'

They didn't. They bought Rosy's notice.

'Pah!' snorted the King.

But at last a near-sighted gentleman bought the King's picture of a ruined castle because it reminded him of his favourite Uncle George. Someone else bought two more pictures to keep the sun off the wallpaper, and ten more were bought because they had rather nice frames. The Queen had the rest hung in the new dungeons, though this seemed a bit hard on the prisoners.

Finally the King gave the Queen his sketch-book to use as a shopping list.

'I shall give up sketching and painting and stick to ruling the kingdom,' he said. 'It's a lot easier.'

'That's because I'm here to tell you how to do it,' said the Queen. 'And I can't pretend to tell you how to paint pictures.'

'It's about the only thing you don't keep telling me how to do,' said the King.

'Yes,' said the Queen. 'And see what a mess you made of it.'

And with that she swept majestically out.

12

Direful Dragonry

Rat a tat, bangetty bang, bong bong, crash. There was a tremendous thumping and banging on the front door of the royal palace of Incrediblania.

'Whoever can that be?' cried the Queen. 'Not Cousin Carole. She always comes in by the garden door and *will* pick the flowers on the way. Can't be Uncle Henry, he always tells the guards to open the door for him. And it isn't a foreign potentate or we'd have had elephants and trumpet calls and red carpet all over the place days ago.'

Crash! The door flew open and in rushed a tremendous dragon, breathing multi-coloured fire and scorching the curtains.

'How dare you rush in like that,' shouted the King, secretly ringing for the guards, but the dragon had knocked them all flat on the way in.

'I don't know any other way to rush in,' said the dragon, blowing the cobwebs off the chandelier with a puff of purple smoke. 'I've come to claim half the kingdom before you start offering it to people to slay me. I don't care to be slain; it spoils my appetite.'

'B-b-b-but you can't do that,' gasped the King. 'Dragons can't claim half kingdoms.'

'*I* can,' said the dragon. 'And if I don't get it I'll

stamp on the lot like that.' He stamped on three chairs and a sofa.

Before the King had time to say anything else, there was another thunderous knocking and the door flew open as a second dragon galloped in, scorching the

back scales of the first dragon with some instant high speed flame of his own.

'You went out and slew a dragon last Thursday week,' this dragon shouted at the King. 'Give me half the kingdom as compenwhatzname, or I'll eat you with tomato sauce. And I'd stamp on the palace, only I've got corns.'

'Outrageous!' shouted the Queen.

'My name's Sizzleflame, not Rageous,' the dragon yelled back, 'and don't you go trying to out me.'

'I . . .' the Queen began, when in tore a third dragon with dirtier smoke and different coloured flame, plus fancy stars.

'Dragons of the world unite!' it shouted. 'No more rewards for slaying us. We demand half the kingdom each.' He lashed his tail round and knocked over a photo of the Queen's best friend, which the King had been trying to lose for ages.

'Now, now, now, now,' said the King. 'You can't do that you know. There are three of you and you can't have three half kingdoms. It isn't arithmetic.'

'Shove it through the computer,' said the third dragon. 'Anyway I don't want half the kingdom, I want all of it.'

'Here, I say, stop that!' shouted the first dragon. 'Fair do's all round. You can't have all the kingdom. I want half of it. I was here first.'

'What about me?' roared the second dragon. 'If you chop the kingdom up into three, we'll all get less than what's offered for slaying us. I want it all. You two go away.'

Then there was the most frightful flaming argument among the three dragons. Smoke of all colours went up, steam sizzled about, flames licked the walls, and the palace shook. Pictures came down. The guards got up, grabbed their swords and ran away.

The Queen was all for calling Princess Rosy to bring her magic crayons and draw a dragon-abolishing thing, but the Princess was busy thinking about drawing a baby with them, so that it would pop up all ready kicking and crying and save her having one herself.

The dragon fight went raging on. Pictures flew here and there, curtains went up in smoke. Furniture became exceedingly second-hand.

The King rushed out and fetched the Court Magician.

'Cast a spell,' he shouted. 'Decant an incantation. Do something to stop all this and get rid of those dragons.'

But all the Magician could do was wave his hands and produce a flag of Incrediblania, which a dragon swallowed though it gave him hiccoughs.

'I can't get rid of the dragons, Majesty,' he shouted in the King's ear. 'But come out here where it's quieter. I've an idea.'

'It had better be a top-of-the-pops-double-sided-twelve-band-super-stereo-idea with bells on!' cried the King.

Out in the corridor the Magician explained his idea to the King.

'Let's get the wicked Count Bakwerdz out of the dungeons,' he said, 'and tell him he must either think of a way of saving the kingdom from the dragons, or be thrown to them himself. That way we either save the kingdom, or get rid of the wicked Count for ever, so we can't lose.'

'Right,' said the King. 'Fetch the wicked Count and I hope we can count on him.'

Not stopping to laugh at the King's rather suet

pudding joke, the Magician fetched the Count and the King told him what he had to do.

'Ah, oh yes, of course, Majesty,' said the Count, wondering how he could think up a way of saving the kingdom from the dragons and getting it for himself. 'It'll take some doing,' he thought. 'But I'm clever, I am. Dastardly, that's me.' Then he suddenly had an idea and told the King about it.

The King was delighted.

'Jolly good!' he said. 'That'll do it. Let's go back and tell the dragons.'

Telling the dragons took a bit of doing as they were still fighting and it was rather like talking nicely to a clump of Saracen tanks with all guns firing. But at last the dragons tired themselves out and sat in a row against the wall with their tongues hanging out and panting like unreasonable road-mending machines.

'Listen, my good dragons,' said the King in his most marzipan-and-ice-cream voice, which he usually kept for trying to persuade the Queen to let him do as he liked. 'We have thought of a way of solving the problem so that distributing the kingdom is fair to all of you.'

'What's the catch?' snarled dragon number one.

'No cheating!' cried dragon number two.

'Let's hear it then,' said dragon three.

The King put his crown straight and said:

'We propose that there shall be a grand dragon race and whoever wins the race shall have half the kingdom.'

'No,' roared dragon one. 'Half's no good. I want it all!'

'Don't be so unreasonable,' said dragon two. 'Their Majesties must have somewhere to live. Anyway half the kingdom's enough. All of it would be too much work. Think of all the weeding.'

'Let's have the race,' said dragon three, who reckoned he was pretty nippy when it came to running.

'Oh, all right,' agreed dragon one.

'Good,' said the King. 'Then shall we say Thursday week at two o'clock?'

'And mind you get a good crowd to watch,' roared dragon one. 'I like to hear a lot of people cheering, it gives me an appetite.'

Then the dragons got up and went away. The King got in men in overalls to get the place tidied up, and the Queen had an enormous tea with cream buns, as she said this was the best treatment for shock.

But good gracious! What sort of an idea was this, the wicked Count Bakwerdz had suggested? One of the dragons was bound to win and that would mean Incrediblania would lose half its kingdom. Outrageous!

But there was a teeny bit more to the Count's idea than the King had told the dragons. No cheating, of course, but still just a little something. But, oh dear and alas, etc., there was also something the wicked Count hadn't told the King. Here was double-dyed cheating of the topmost bottom of craftiness. It was a fearful plan within a dastardly plan. The Count had schemed to save the kingdom from the dragons, oh yes, but in doing so he was going to get it for himself. Or at least half of it, which was three-quarters too much for the wicked Count to get.

Thursday week dawned exactly right to the minute in spite of British summer time and weather forecasts. It was fine and sunny with no wind, and the going looked just right for dragon racing.

By a quarter to two the crowds had gathered, the ice-cream men and hot dog retailers had sold out, and the excitement was more intense than Cup Final, Derby Day, the Eurovision Song Contest and Miss World all put together.

The three dragons arrived with their scales pulled up nice and tight so that they could run fast.

'Here I say,' said dragon one, 'who's that fourth dragon?'

'Oh,' said the king, 'he arrived a few days after you and we thought it only fair to let him compete.'

'Well he doesn't look as if he can run much,' said dragon two.

'I could give him a mile start and win easily,' sneered dragon three.

'Right,' said the King. 'Well that's all settled then, we can begin the race.'

But who was that fourth dragon who had so mysteriously arrived from goodness knows where? Ha! That was Count Bakwerdz's idea. It wasn't a dragon at all. It was an imitation one made of painted linoleum and sticks, which covered a whole row of the King's guards mounted on super-fast bicycles.

'It can beat any dragon,' said the Count. 'They won't have a chance. Then you can award half the kingdom prize to your own mechanical dragon and still keep it.'

'But isn't that cheating a bit?' Princess Sonia had asked.

'Of course it is,' said the King. 'But when dragons come demanding half kingdoms for nothing, I think you have a perfect right to cheat just a little bit.'

The dragons were lined up for the start. The crowd were so excited several of them couldn't eat the peanuts and potato crisps and candyfloss and ice cream and buns and sandwiches and bananas they'd brought with them, because crowds always get very hungry whenever they watch anything.

'Now remember,' said the King to the dragons, 'no flying allowed. This is a running race. Nobody is to get up in the air about it.'

'Agreed,' snorted the dragons, pawing the ground, while several of the crowd got very much up in the air, climbing on one another's shoulders and into trees to get a better view.

'Ready?' cried the King.

Bang! The Captain of the Guard fired a cannon and the great dragon race began.

Thrumpetty, thrumpetty, boom, bonk, thrrrrump! The claws of the four dragons beat the ground. *Zimmy, zimmy, zim, zim, zim.* The wheels of the bicycles inside the King's dragon spun along. Flames and smoke shot out in front of the dragons, dust rose behind them. The crowd stopped eating and held their breaths. Eyes bulged, hair rose on end.

Dragon two began gaining on the others. Then dragon three put on a spurt and clawed its way ahead.

'Ra, ra, yah, yah, hurray!' yelled the crowd, not knowing who to shout for, but simply having to shout for something.

The King's dragon was doing well. The guards were pedalling like mad. All three dragons were snout to snout. Then, as they came round a bend, dragon one drew ahead. But dragon three was hot on his tail, particularly as his fiery breath began scorching dragon one's rear end. The King's dragon gained ground then lost it again. Dragon two crept up on the others. Again it was snout to snout. Ten duchesses fainted, but came unfainted at once so as not to miss anything. The two Princesses and Princes clutched one another and hoped the King's dragon would win in case it didn't and the half kingdom the winning dragon got cut off their back gardens.

Smoke and flames. Dust and excitement. Dragon one was in front again. No, no, dragon three was overtaking him. Dragon two was nowhere. Yes he was, he was gaining again. But hurray, the King's dragon came up on the off side. *Zim, zim, zim,* it spun along. It drew ahead and was soon half a length in front of the leading dragon. Dragon one made a spurt, but fell back. Dragon three came on again. But the King's dragon forged on. Now it was three lengths ahead.

'Hurray, hurray, wow, wow, hurray!' yelled the crowd, throwing their hats in the air and never mind what they came down on.

'We're winning, we're winning!' shouted the King, then his braces bust in the excitement, and he had to put his hands in his trouser pockets and couldn't wave them.

But, good gracious, what was this? A fifth dragon suddenly appeared. Quite a small one, but terrifically fast and blowing out flames, not from his mouth as every respectable dragon is expected to do, but from his tail.

It was the wicked Count Bakwerdz, disguised as a dragon and riding a hidden motor bike he had stolen while the owner was listening to top pop tunes inside his crash helmet.

Pop, pop, popetty pop, zim, zim, zim, roarrrrr, bang, bang, whizizizizziz. The wicked Count's dragon shot past all the other dragons and swung round in front of the King's dragon. The other dragons would win. Half the kingdom was lost. But no, no, no, dreadfuller than that. The wicked Count was going to win. He would get half the kingdom, which might be even worse than the dragons getting it because then he'd start scheming to get the other half.

Crash, bang. The wicked Count's dragon hit the front of the King's dragon and shot off ahead. The next moment the King's dragon was all in bits. Bicycles and guards and bits of linoleum and sticks were all over the place.

'Oh, my goodness, we're undone!' groaned the

King, taking his hands out of his pockets to wring them, and then his trousers fell down because he really was undone, owing to busted braces.

'Oh, oh, oh, dreadful situation!' moaned the Queen.

Princess Sonia rushed forward and fastened the King's trousers up with safety pins.

Alas, alas, Incrediblania was beaten. Half the kingdom would have to go to the dragon. Oh, oh, oh!'

But ha! The wicked Count's dragon was far ahead, when suddenly the front wheel of his motor bike hit a big stone. *Boom, crash.* He shot up in the air and landed with an explosion that blew the hats off all the people, who'd stopped throwing them up now the King wasn't winning.

The wicked Count was out of the race, hurray! But oh, oh no, un-hurray. Dragon number two flashed past the post, the winner.

Just then the wicked Count Bakwerdz came hobbling up with half a motor bike wheel round his neck, his dragon costume in rags and smuts all over his face.

'Objection!' he shouted. 'Objection!'

'Objection!' shouted the King. 'It is we who object. First you have your mechanical dragon idea for us to win and then you deliberately fouled us and lost us the race.'

The dragons came panting up, their tongues hanging out like red blankets on a washing line and you could hardly see them for ,steam.

'All right, all right,' groaned the King. 'You've won. I must concede half the kingdom. Let us decide which half you are to have.'

But the dragons shook their heads.

'We don't, puff puff, want any of your, pant, puff, kingdom,' said dragon two.

'You don't what?' gasped the King, thinking his ears had stopped working.

'We don't want half the kingdom,' said dragon two. 'We reckon we shouldn't know what to do with it. We're too big to get into the cafes and theatres and bingo halls, so what sort of fun could we have? And how could you expect a dragon to run half a kingdom. We don't know anything about drains, or repairing roads, or collecting rates, or delivering letters, or enforcing speed limits, or not letting people loiter with intent to commit felonies.'

'I don't understand,' gasped the King.

'We've all enjoyed the race so much,' said dragon two, 'that we want to stop here and have dragon races every week. You just give us a little corner of the kingdom to live in. We'll be no trouble. We're vegetarians, so we shan't want any beautiful princesses sacrificed and we might even help Your Majesty to defend the kingdom in case of invasion.'

The King didn't know what to say. Even the Queen was speechless for the first time in her reign.

Then the King thought of what to say.

'Excellent, my good dragons,' he said, 'and to reward you for your reasonable attitude you shall have that castle to live in,' he pointed to the grim, grey castle of the wicked Count Bakwerdz, 'and Count Bakwerdz shall wait on you and look after you.'

So that was that. A fitting punishment for the wicked

Count and one likely to keep him from scheming and plotting. So the dragons went to live in Count Bakwerdz's castle, where he had no end of a time getting their meals and doing the cleaning.

And dragon races were held every Thursday afternoon. That not only solved Incrediblania's dragon problem, but the money people paid as they flocked to see the dragon races every week enabled the kingdom to have comprehensive schools, metricated milk bottles, non-paying beds in hospitals and other modern improvements.